William Pilkington

Life Sketch of the Rev. Walter Briscombe

William Pilkington

Life Sketch of the Rev. Walter Briscombe

ISBN/EAN: 9783337393649

Printed in Europe, USA, Canada, Australia, Japan

Cover: Foto ©Raphael Reischuk / pixelio.de

More available books at **www.hansebooks.com**

LIFE SKETCH

OF THE

Rev. WALTER BRISCOMBE.

BY W. PILKINGTON,

AUTHOR OF

"The Makers of Preston Methodism and The Relation of Methodism to the Temperance Movement," etc.

WITH PHOTO-ENGRAVING OF THE REV. WALTER BRISCOMBE.

PRESTON:
Published by W. PILKINGTON, 101, Friargate.
1891.

PREFACE.

The following book is the outcome of a scheme to raise £4,000 in the Preston Wesley Circuit, to commemorate the Centenary of the death of John Wesley.

In addition to the help derived from a subscription list, it was proposed to work up in aid of the scheme a large Bazaar. To awaken and sustain an interest in it, a monthly perodical was published for the preceding six months, called *The Bazaar Times*.

The editor, entertaining the opinion that a brief life sketch of the popular superintendent of the circuit, who had greatly aided the scheme and encouraged the workers in it, would be highly acceptable to the readers of the paper, sought an interview with him for the purpose. The reverend gentleman was very reluctant to appear in such personal prominence in *The Bazaar Times*, but on assuring him that it would gratify a large number of his flock, increase the sale of *The Bazaar Times*, and indirectly contribute to the success of the great schemo itself to raise £4,000, the only weak place in his nature was touched and he was induced to consent. But the numerous interesting incidents which the writer gathered from a variety of sources made his original purpose impossible, if anything like justice had to be done to the subject of the sketch and the cause he represented. He therefore sought another interview with the reverend gentleman in regard to this enlarged project, and having obtained a somewhat reluctant consent, had the pleasure of announcing, in the last issue of *The Bazaar Times,* his intention of publishing the present volume.

To trace the early history; to mark the influence of incidents leading to success; and to record the events of a life distinguished by a steady devotion to philanthropy and Christian duty has been to the author a labour of love, a task of delight, and a matter of absorbing interest. If the reader, in pursuing its pages, receives but a tithe of the pleasure and profit attained by the writer the author will be amply rewarded. The work contains, in addition to the early record of his life, a general sketch of his history in the eleven circuits in which he has travelled since he entered the Methodist ministry.

W. PILKINGTON.

Friargate, Preston,
Dec., 1891.

LIFE SKETCH

OF THE

Rev. WALTER BRISCOMBE.

Men who live, think and work for the welfare of others, become gradually enshrined in the hearts and memories of their fellows. Identifying their talents with the exigencies of the times, they trace out for themselves careers of unostentatious self-denial and beneficence ; and become unconsciously, renowned. An inexpressible charm surrounds their names and the localities which have been hallowed by their presence. Their virtues and their deeds are as seeds sown, from whence spring up others, who are actuated by similar motives, and who strive in a spirit of emulation to serve their generation. The most noble and useful lives are not always those which abound in exciting incidents or adventures. The ship that speeds over calm waters leaves a broad and widening track, fringed with light; it is otherwise with the explosive that rends and devastates all around.

It is the noiseless process by which nature produces the fruits and flowers of the earth. As in nature, so with men. The life of the subject of our

sketch is outwardly a quiet one. His genial disposition, fair-mindedness, and vigorous ability are
devoted to the good cause of bettering the lives and
brightening the homes of the people. In our
endeavours to secure a complete record of the life
of our esteemed superintendent minister, the Rev.
Walter Briscombe, we have been obliged to supple-
ment our outside resources of information by the
American method of interviewing.

We shall endeavour to narrate as nearly in his
own words and phrases as we are able to do, but
they fall much flatter in print than when told in
the excellent style of Mr. Briscombe himself. In
reply to our numerous inquiries about his

EARLY LIFE AND SCHOOL DAYS,
we elicited the information we now present to our
readers. The subject of our present attention was
born in the year 1836, at Whitelee, in the parish of
Batley, Yorkshire, at a point of the parish bordering
on Birstall, which was the head of one of the most
influential of the early circuits of Methodism in the
days of John Wesley. His parents were pewholders,
and regular attendants at the Birstall Wesleyan
Chapel, and he himself attended both chapel and the
Sunday school connected with it from the age of about
five years. He remembers the rebuilding of the Birstall
chapel in the year 1846, and recollects hearing the
Rev. George Highfield preach the last sermon in
the old chapel early in the same year. This venerable man was received into the ministry of the

Methodist Church in the year 1786 by the Rev. John Wesley. He had preached the first sermon in the old chapel fifty years before, and though at that time nearly 90 years of age he was desired to preach the last sermon in it, and consented. Mr. Briscombe was then 10 years of age, and remembers how, after the service, he walked to a place in the chapel yard where the aged minister of Christ was to pass, and stood to gaze upon his venerable countenance. The aged saint saw him and some other boys in this observant attitude, and with smiling look and gentle words said, " Come hither, my boys, and let me put my hands upon your heads and give you my blessing." The other boys, through some cause or other, held back, but he, as desired, walked up to the venerated man and received both the imposition of his hands and his patriarchal blessing. He not only treasures the event as a signal honour of his boyhood, but recognising the devoutness of the man who bestowed it, and his own reverent sincerity in receiving it, he regards it as one of those divine channels through which God ministered to him an ennobling influence, and imparted a spiritual blessing.

He attended this Sunday school until his 16th year, when he left his father's house for a few years to live in Leeds. In those days and in that school it was the uniform custom for the children to rise in the class according to their excellence in reading and answering questions. If a boy pronounced a word wrongly the others below him, in rotation, were requested to correct the error, and he who did so took his place. The same rule was observed also in answering questions on the lesson proposed by the teacher. Having been favoured with a day school education much above what was common in those days, he was generally at the head of his class. To be at the head of the class for three Sundays in succession entitled a scholar to be removed into the next highest class. Following this custom he was soon in the first class of a large Sunday school numbering between 400 and 500 scholars. He was much the youngest scholar in that class, but on account of his better educational advantages he commonly obtained the top place. The teacher of this highest boys' class, Mr. John Nussey, was a gentleman of good social position, both by birth, education, wealth, and high Christian character. On not a few occasions, when the subject of our narrative was first in the class, he would ask a question beginning with the second youth in the class, and going down with it, when unanswered, to the bottom, he would then say, " Come, Briscombe, tell them what it is." This was said with so confident an expectation of a correct reply that a failure to meet the case was as great a humiliation as the success was an honour.

His earliest recollection of day school life was attending a dame school kept by an elderly woman in a cottage not far from his father's house. His

only remembrance of it is an incident of his being
called upon to read to a visitor to whom the school-
mistress wished to give a specimen of the attain-
ments of her young scholars. Some sort of commendation was then given which seems to have
been the reason why a boy of four years old has
remembered it from so early a period. Soon after
this he was sent to another dame school, supposed
to be somewhat higher in its teachings, at a small
village called Carlinghow. He was attending this
school when the most calamitous event of his life
occurred,

The Death of his Mother.

He was then just over six years of age, but he
vividly remembers receiving her last kiss on the
morning on which she died. He then left for
Sunday school and chapel, little thinking that his
mother would be dead before he returned. He
recollects on entering the house immediately
running upstairs to the bedroom where he had left
her, and finding neither herself nor anyone else in
the room he ran down as quickly, calling out,
" Where is my mother?" His father, who had
just come out of another room, took him up in his
arms, telling him that his mother was dead, and
took him into the room where she was laid out.
His unutterably forlorn feeling on that occasion,
with its accompanying grief, can only be known by
those who have lost a loving mother in early life.
Often afterwards, as he returned from school, he

looked up at the window from which his mother had frequently looked out to watch for his return, and in his imagination he often thought he saw her smiling face there, which quickened both the beating of his heart and the pace of his footsteps, but his speedier entrance only the sooner dispelled the illusion by reminding him that he was now motherless. Not long after his mother's death an incident occurred which revealed the strength of his early religious principles. The housekeeper who used to put him to bed, thinking he was too long in saying his prayers, and wishing to see him in bed before she went down stairs, lifted him from his knees into bed, covered him, and took the light away. He was at that time exceedingly timid in the dark, but he feared to fall asleep before he had finished his prayers. The strength of conviction rose above this terror of darkness, and he quickly crept out of bed, knelt down in the dark and solitary room, finished his prayers, returned to bed, and at once fell asleep. Considering his youth and fears he regards this as an act of moral courage that God graciously approved. Having stayed at the dame school till his father thought he had learned as much as the mistress could teach he was removed to a much superior school at Birstall, taught by a Mrs. Hopper. It was a boarding school for young ladies, but open also to young boys as day scholars. Here he continued for a time, but his leaving was hastened by a painful occurrence. A large dog was

kept by the principal of the school, which used to
be locked up during school hours in a roomy place
underneath a part of the house. On running out
of the school-room one day the dog, which had
been loose, flew after him and bit his leg. His
father was so grieved that he immediately took him
away from the school. Finding that his son had
reached that standard of education which was
required before he could become a scholar in the
Batley Grammar School, he forthwith took the
necessary steps to place him there. The school was
about two miles distant, and he was then only in
his ninth year. He attended, however, with great
regularity. Left motherless at six years of
age, he was bereft of that anxious watching,
the loss of which is sometimes so harmful,
but he had an inalienable heritage of sterling
qualities and shining gifts from the mother who
was not destined to live and rejoice in her son's
career. The lively and ruddy-cheeked boy was full
of high and hearty impulses. It is interesting to
trace the first ideas of young people and to observe
their influence on after life. When Mr. Briscombe
was about eight years of age he was very fond of
reading the old Methodist magazines, several of
which were in his home. In every monthly number
there was a portrait of some Methodist minister
and underneath his name was added, "Preacher
of the Gospel." On one occasion Walter stood up
on an arm chair, some of his brothers being present,

and with childish attempt at preaching introduced his subject with saying, "I'm the preacher of the Gospel." The outburst of laughter that this undesigned prophecy excited among his brothers, together with much after teasing, fixed the incident unfadingly in his memory.

"Robinson Crusoe" was a very popular book which he read through with avidity in his early days. In a neighbour's house where he was accustomed to visit, on one occasion, when he was speaking about the book, the neighbour said "that it was quite a true account of Robinsou Crusoe, because it gave the very place where he was born." When about the same age he read through the "Pilgrim's Progress." Thinking he had accomplished a great work, he ran to his father and said, with an air of triumph, "Father, I've read the 'Pilgrim's Progress,' quite through." His father quickly replied, "Well! and do you understand it?" Walter made no answer, but, turning away, began to consider what his father meant. He had read the book as a literal occurrence, but by suggestive aids he soon gathered a conception of its allegorical meaning. There was a tolerable collection of books in Mr. Briscombe's house, and his young boy largely read them, especially those which suited his mental appetite. Barclay's Dictionary was a specially favourite book, a sort of small encyclopædia containing, in addition to its explanation of words, condensed accounts of notable men, important cities, and remarkable events. On long winter evenings, when gas was unknown, his father often read aloud some entertaining or instructive books, such as " Tim Bobbin, or sketches of humorous characters in the Lancashire dialect," " History of France," &c. Sometimes his father would question him on grammar, and would draw him out in parsing, and if there were any doubtful points in regard to parts of speech, it was always settled by an appeal to Barclay's or Walker's dictionaries. For seven years he worked well at his school, making steady advance in learning. At the close of his school life he had a fair knowledge of French and Latin, and was well up in grammar, arithmetic, mensuration, &c. He remembers a farmer coming to him when he was a school boy to help him to calculate the cubic feet of hay in a haystack which he had bargained to sell. The measurement being taken, the farmer sold the stack according to the calculation he made, as based upon the measurement given.

A story is told of a gathering of Highland clans in the long ago, when the proper place of each chief was as jealously insisted upon as is often now-a-days done in the dying "dignity" of a coroner's court. When the seven chiefs came to sit down at table, a dispute at once arose as to which of them should occupy the seat of honour. The wrangle was at its height when in walked Macdonald. " What's the difficulty ? " asked that chieftain in the dialect of the period; "whence all this disputation ? "

And when he was told it was over who should preside, he at once sat down, exclaiming, "Wherever the Macdonald sits, that's the head of the table!" So it was with young Briscombe, whether in the Sunday or day school, a dame or grammar school, wherever he sat was the head of the class. The villagers were not slow to recognise his many promising qualities, and many anticipated for him a successful career.

Mr. Briscombe's father had been fairly successful in business, and retired early from it, having made a small competency. Being a well-read man, and having a great admiration for learning, he was wishful that his youngest son should qualify for one of the professions. His original purpose was to keep him at the Grammar School until he was 18 years of age, and then send him to some college that might best answer his further purposes. But when the youth had entered on his sixteenth year one or two events, small in themselves, largely modified these intentions. All his most intimate school companions had gradually left the school for business or other callings, and on his return, after one of the holidays, he felt a sort of sentimental solitude in the severance of so many schoolboy associations. While under the influence of this sentiment an elder brother, who occupied a good position in a large wholesale grocery establishment in Leeds, paid a visit to the parental home. He urged his younger brother to leave school and enter

the same establishment, there being then an opening, and the principal having expressed a wish to
receive his younger brother. This persuasion
induced him to consent. His father was consulted,
and he agreed to leave the matter to his own
decision, but reserving several conditions, viz., that
he should not go unless the principal consented to
release him at eighteen years of age, and that he
should not be at all bound by indenture, a course
which was then uniformly adopted. These conditions were mutually agreed upon, and for a few
years he entered into business life. The College
to which his father designed to send him belonged
to the Church of England, in the diocese of Durham,
and was for the training of schoolmasters, but did
not admit youths until they were eighteen years of
age. It was considered that a few years at business
might add variety to his experience of life without
seriously interfering with his progress in learning.
When his step-mother went to discharge his school
bill after he had left, the Rev. Joseph Senior, LL.D.,
the head master, after stating his regret at the
sudden removal of the boy, expressed the opinion
that it would have been more suitable to his attain-
ments to have prepared him for one of the professions, than send him into commercial life.

BUSINESS LIFE.

It was in the year 1851, so memorable for the
beginning of public Exhibitions, that Walter first
entered upon learning a business. The staff of

the establishment consisted of the master, three journeymen, three apprentices, and two porters. Young Briscombe attended to the customary duties of his position, and in his leisure hours kept up in a limited measure his school studies and general reading. He had not been there many months when, through the kindness of his father and the consent of his master, he was permitted to visit the original Crystal Palace, at London, the first of all the great National Exhibitions which have since then successively taken place. This, to him, was so far the most notable event of his life. Railways were then only in their infancy, and the farthest distance Walter had travelled from his native place was to Scarborough. The prospect of travelling 200 miles to the great Metropolis of England and visiting the world-renowned Exhibition roused his imagination to ideas of fairy grandeur. As he passed through the magic world of art and science, that resplendent structure glistening in the sun and adorned with the finest collection of useful and beautiful objects, it was to him a new world. The great magnificence of the sight left such a strong impression on his mind that, though forty years have passed, the vividness of the scene is but little impaired. All the surroundings of the week he spent in London, comprising sails on the river, rides in the city, and visits to the great sights, only added to his delighted wonder.

It is needless to say that he returned home with a mind enlarged by a more practical knowledge of the world and enriched by a new kind of information gathered from realities on which he had gazed. Walter now settled down to his duties of everyday life, and sought to be worthy of the approval of those under whom he served. With the exception of an occasional friction between himself and a youth in the establishment about his own age, the time he served in the business passed over agreeably. The friction referred to was only occasional, and in a year or two died out, resulting at last in a sincere friendship.

After being in this establishment about a year, his former religious convictions became intensified under the ministrations of the Rev. John Rattenbury, at the Brunswick Chapel, Leeds (where he had taken a sitting), and exerted the greatest influence in leading him to an avowed decision for Christ and a personal union with his people. A sermon by that minister from the text: " Wilt Thou not from this time cry unto me, My Father, Thou art the guide of my youth" (Jer. iii. 4), moved him very powerfully, and contributed largely to his determination to seek for a conscious sense of the Divine favour, and avow his Christian discipleship by connecting himself with the Methodist Church.

CONVERSION.

Being very reticent on religious matters, though thinking keenly about them, he refrained from conversing on the subject, and sought privately to make his peace with God. This course prolonged his spiritual anxiety and delayed the reception of that blessed assurance of God's favour which would in all likelihood have been accelerated by the judicious counsel of some experienced Christian friend. After many anxious doubts and fears, the joys of salvation were realised. One evening he retired early to his bedroom and knelt down to read the Holy Scriptures for inspiration and instruction, and lifted up his soul in prayer for saving grace. Having read many remarkable cases of conversion, and having heard in love-feasts startling processes by which great sinners had been brought to God, he fell into the error of supposing that some great convulsion would seize hold of his spiritual nature and that some rapturous excitement would follow as the sign of the Divine favour. He had not then sufficiently learned the diversity of Divine operations in the processes that lead to a conscious sense of salvation. The conversion of the Philippian gaoler was the typical instance which he had heard related at love-feasts, and with a deep sense of his own unworthiness he formed the opinion that he might undergo such an earthquake shock, and experience immediately after it an ecstatic sensation of joy. But the crisis of his conscious acceptance with God was neither preceded by violent convulsions of mind nor followed by thrilling sensations of joy. God spoke to him in the "still small voice," not in thunder. The gentle and gracious change that took place in Lydia, "whose heart the Lord opened," reflected the mode of the Divine operation in this case. Having closed the Bible and extinguished the light on the evening referred to, he again knelt down for reflection and prayer. He began to think of cases of conversion which had been related that seemed as if they had heard a voice saying, "Thy sins are forgiven thee," and he exclaimed, "O that God would permit me to hear such a Divine voice in this room! I would then regard it as a proof of his pardoning mercy." He thought of St. Paul's conversion when "there shined round about him a light from heaven," and he said, "O that God would let such a light shine in this room now, and I would regard it as the sign of His favour and the assurance of my salvation!" But no voice fell upon his ears, nor was any light revealed to his eyes. Again he began to ponder as to what the reasons might be which intercepted such a Divine manifestation to his spirit. He thought, "I have endeavoured to forsake all evil, and resolved, with God's help, to obey all His commands; I have sincerely confessed my sins and humbly entreated the forgiveness of them; why does He not impart to me, as to so many others, the assurance of His favour?" A thought then occurred, suggested no doubt by the Divine Spirit:—"Why do I desire to hear a supernatural voice or to see a supernatural light? Does it not spring from my distrust of God's promises? If God has promised this pardon to all those who comply with His required conditions, and, seeing that I have sincerely endeavoured to do so, why dare I not believe that, according to His promise, He pardons me?" This view gave spiritual insight into the subject, and whilst yet on his knees he frequently exclaimed, " Then, Lord, without any supernatural voice or light, I take Thee at Thy word, and because I have complied with Thy conditions I believe now that, for Christ's sake, Thou dost pardon me." This firm reliance upon the promises composed his anxious mind into a tranquil state. He regarded this experience as the Divine message to his soul, and has ever since maintained that conviction. The senior apprentice, who was already a member of the Methodist Church, invited him to a class meeting. He accepted the invitation, realised its importance, felt the difficulty of taking up his cross in confessing Christ before men, attended the class with great regularity, received from it valuable aid, which enriched his religious experience and established his Christian life. Mr. Briscombe having completed his 18th year, the period when, according to his father's agreement, he was to leave the business for the purpose of going to a training college for Church schoolmasters, his new associations had changed his decision. In his tenderness of conscience he thought that he ought not to set aside the unvarying past custom of all the previous apprentices who had served until they were twenty-one. He judged that on the ground of business honour he ought to remain for the same length of time as the former apprentices, notwithstanding that they were legally bound and he was not; and that in his case there had been an express verbal agreement between the master and his father that he should leave at eighteen. He desired also to keep himself in connection with these Methodist surroundings and new associations. Mr. Briscombe became a Sunday school teacher, tract distributor, sick visitor, and an attendant at the Rev. Ed. Lightwood's Bible Class. Under these influences he resolved to remain the full term.

FIRST APPEARANCE ON THE PUBLIC PLATFORM.

His first attempt at public speaking was the reading of a prize essay on "How to make Sabbath School teaching effective." The Sunday school teachers of the four Leeds circuits had a Union for promoting their efficiency. Competitive subjects were announced, and the teachers were invited to write on them. The successful essays were read at the annual meeting. Young Briscombe tried one year and failed, but the year following he tried again and succeeded. There were four different subjects for competitive essays, and he took the one above mentioned. The other three essayists competed on other subjects. It was a formidable undertaking for him when under twenty years of age, and of highly nervous susceptibility, he was called upon to read his essay in the presence of 400 teachers, many of whom were gentlemen of culture and position, and he the youngest of all the essayists. By the force of circumstances he happened to sit at the table where a select number of the leading gentlemen sat, who, while partaking of tea, began to discuss the subject of the essayists, not knowing that the youth beside them was one of the number. When they commenced with the subject of our sketch, an elderly gentleman said, "As for this Mr. Briscombe, I don't know him, but one of my sons knows him well. He is very young and, I understand, rather timid. His essay is reported to be a good one, but I fear in this large room he will not be heard." At this point of his remarks he flew off at a tangent, and began to philosophise on the art of speaking so as to be heard by a large audience, little thinking of the service he was unconsciously rendering to an unfledged speaker who that night was about to try his wings for the first time. He said that the secret of being heard did not consist so much in a loud voice as in a distinct one, and that if a speaker dropped his voice at the last letter of a word or the last word of a sentence he would not be well heard. He quoted some distinguished public speaker of that day who confirmed the opinion he had expressed. At this point the tea tables began to be cleared, and young Briscombe retired to some quiet place to familiarise himself with his essay and reflect on what he had heard. The meeting was constituted, and, in due course, he was called upon to read his essay. He read it with a distinctness that enabled him to be heard, as the applause of the hearers often indicated. He was not able to add much to the force of the matter by the gaze of the eye, for he had not the confidence that enabled him to look his audience in the face.

At twenty-one years of age, by desire of his father, he returned home, leaving business for a more congenial occupation. This incident reminds us of a story in the course of the feuds which raged for some time between the Scotch Kings and their powerful subjects the Earls of Douglas. A *rencontre* took place one day on the outskirts of a Border village, when the King's adherents were worsted. One of them took refuge in the village smithy, where he hastily disguised himself, and, donning a spare leather apron, pretended to be engaged in assisting the smith with his work, when a party of the Douglas followers rushed in. They glanced at the pretended workman at the anvil, and observed him deliver a blow upon it so unskilfully that the hammer-shaft broke in his hand. On this, one of the Douglas men rushed at him, calling out " Ye're nae smyth !" The assailed man seized his sword, which lay conveniently at hand, and defended himself so vigorously that he shortly killed his assailant, while the smith brained another with his hammer; and a party of the King's men having come to their help, the rest were speedily overpowered. The Royal forces then rallied, and their temporary defeat was converted into a victory. Such is said to be the traditional origin of the Scotch family of Naesmyth. It was patent to the father of the subject of this sketch, and also to other friends, that Walter Briscombe was "nae" grocer, but that he was destined for higher work. Hence he was "called back" from the grocery establishment, and his father still suggested the work of a schoolmaster, to which Walter consented, with a view of greater facility for study as a means of preparing for the ministry. A school-room was constructed out of an existing building in his father's possession, which was soon filled with scholars from the village and neighbourhood. Being supported by his father, he did not feel the strain of the limited income of a village school, and had leisure to receive lessons in Greek and study theology as a means of equipment for the ministry. Shortly after returning home he was called to the offices of local preacher and class leader. During the period that Mr. Briscombe was on probation as a local preacher he fell into a doctrinal error respecting the hypostatic union of the two natures in the one person of our Lord. In working out the idea of the two-fold nature of Christ from the standpoint of his own thinking, he fell into the error of supposing that the Divine nature of the Son of God stood in the place of a human spirit to our Lord's body. The error, which was an old heresy advocated by some teachers in the earliest ages of

Christianity, regarded our Lord as having a human body but not a human spirit, and assumed that the Divine spirit nature within was the only spirit that animated Him. He happened to preach this doctrine in his trial sermon as a local preacher, and to maintain it at his theological examination. This delayed his coming on full plan for a season. Upon being advised to read Pearson on the Creed he did so, and, with more light, soon perceived and abandoned the error, recognising that, in His dual nature, Jesus Christ was both perfect God and perfect man, both natures being joined in one person. This episode delayed his entrance into the ministry at least one year. This error was probably overruled for his good in leading him to greater investigation of the doctrines of the Christian faith. They have a saying in Cumberland that when the bairns reach a certain age they are thrown on to the house-rigg, and that those who stick on are made thatchers of, while those who fall off are sent to St. Bees to be made parsons of. Had this test been applied to Mr. Briscombe, when a boy, he would have been classed with those who fell off.

A Call to the Ministry.

His natural gift of oratory and earnest youthful piety marked him out for the pulpit, and he was called, when 24 years of age, to the Methodist ministry. His excellent early education, which had been diligently improved during the three years he taught a private school, caused him to pass his examinations successfully, and to be received as a minister on probation without the usual period of a college training.

FIRST CIRCUIT.

His first appointment was to engage in home mission work at the Ebenezer Chapel in the Carver-street Circuit, Sheffield, in the year 1861.

AN EMPTY CHAPEL.

This large chapel, in the midst of a densely populated part of the town, had through various causes nearly lost its congregation. The young pastor struggled with difficulties and disadvantages. To preach to empty pews was out of the question. But the commercial training he received as a grocer gave him tact in approaching men on religious subjects at the very commencement of his ministerial labours. He had the elements in him which have often won a brilliant reputation. He had then, as now, an ardent, impetuous, glowing heart, a mind full of life and activity, and a copious command of language. To fill empty pews requires often a pre-established reputation. The very name of a deserted chapel repels approach. But what of that, the field was open before him. Though not of the school of the prophets, his search after knowledge and earnest piety filled his quiver and gave point and polish to arrows for which his bow was already bent. Away he went into the streets and lanes in the locality of Ebenezer Chapel, and without adopting any sensational method, but chiefly by visiting and preaching in the cottages and sometimes in the open air, his earnest mission work came upon the community of this district with freshness and novelty, and was felt in its sterling truthfulness and life. In a short time the former things passed away, and the young pastor no longer preached to empty pews. The first two years of his ministerial labours had not been wasted, neither had his laborious duties become an excuse for mental inactivity. Here he gave special attention to the study of Hebrew, receiving twice a week for the greater part of two years private lessons from an ex-Jewish Rabbi. His teacher, who at that time was giving lessons to numerous clergymen and ministers in Sheffield, repeatedly said about the close of his two years study that he was the best Hebrew scholar of any whom he had taught in that district. The following year he passed in conjunction with other probationers an examination in Hebrew, and stood at the head of the list, having answered all the questions correctly. His earnest efforts in his first circuit resulted in most encouraging

PROSPERITY.

His mind had thus been quickened to more vigorous study, and his activities during that period had been greatly increased. The deserted chapel, through the well-sustained efforts of Mr. Briscombe and his successors, became one of the best attended places of worship in the town. The young preacher's usefulness won for him noble and enduring fame, and many whom he taught to trust in Christ and keep His commandments regard him with love and reverence. On leaving Sheffield he removed to Grimsby, where he spent another two years of his ministry. His probation then ended, and after examinations in general knowledge and theology, which were deemed most satisfactory, at the Birmingham Conference of 1865 he was ordained to the office of the Methodist ministry.

MARRIAGE.

In a short time after his ordination he was married to Miss Dyson, the eldest daughter of John Dyson, Esq., J.P., Thurgoland, near Sheffield. His acquaintanceship with Miss Dyson was formed several years before, when he exercised his ministry in the Sheffield (Carver-street) Circuit. The engagement subsisted for three years before marriage. The high Christian character, warm religious sympathy, and devoted attention, in a quiet way, to the duties of her position as the wife of a minister, are so many after-proofs of that suitability which Mr. Briscombe had the wisdom to discern when he sought a suitable " help-meet." The marriage ceremony took place in the village chapel of Thurgoland (specially licensed for the occasion) on August 8th, 1865, and the officiating minister was the Rev. Joseph Dyson, uncle of the bride. After a three weeks holiday at Rhyl, Mr. Briscombe and his wife proceeded to Ambleside, then in the

KENDAL CIRCUIT,

where he had been appointed by the preceding Conference. During his residence in this circuit he had special charge of four places in the Lake District, viz., Ambleside, Bowness, Windermere, and Grasmere, but preaching at Kendal, nevertheless, every third Sunday. During this period he had many heavy night walks between Ambleside and the places already mentioned, especially in winter, the worst part of the year, when no public conveyances were available to suit his needs. He was most rigid in keeping his appointments at these places, despite the severity of the weather, and sustained some after-injury to his health on this account. The small chapel at Windermere village was built whilst he was in this circuit, and the superintendent devolved upon him the entire responsibility of looking after it. This was his first effort of the kind, and in a locality where Methodism was feeble was a formid-able undertaking. In addition to recognising God in the spiritual work of the church, he also made the erection of this chapel a special matter of prayer. The pressure of financial difficulty and responsibility in a district where there were few in sympathy with his work, and those few in humble circumstances, led him to earnest prayer that in this matter God would open out his course. Just at the crisis of his anxieties a knock came to his door at nine o'clock one winter's evening. On the door being opened it was found that it was one of the male members of the small society at Windermere, where the chapel was in course of erection. He said, in excited tones, that there was a gentleman at Windermere in dying circumstances who wished to see him as soon as he could about the chapel we were building there. Early next morning Mr. Briscombe journeyed the five miles to see him. The gentleman, who was quite unknown to Mr. Briscombe, made inquiries about the financial needs of the chapel, the erection of which he had witnessed from his sick room, and then wrote out a cheque for £100 for the Building Fund. After religious counsel and prayer, Mr. Briscombe placed the cheque in the bank for the benefit of the Building Fund, and on the following day the sick gentleman died. Whilst recognising that subjects of prayer like this must be offered in deference to God's will, he regarded this case as a proper answer to prayer. The societies and congregations under his charge showed a marked advance, and himself and Mrs. Briscombe enjoyed the high esteem of the whole circuit. Though he was urgently desired to remain three years in the circuit, circumstances induced him to leave at the end of two years. His health had been somewhat impaired by his long night walks to different appointments in a climate very humid in winter. There was no minister's house then at Ambleside, and himself and wife had to live in apartments; and having heard of his intention to leave, the stewards of the neighbouring circuit forwarded him an invitation to become the

SUPERINTENDENT OF ULVERSTON CIRCUIT.

As a minister's house was there provided he accepted

the invitation, which the following Conference ratified,
and in due course he began his ministry in that
circuit, in which the rapidly rising town of Barrow-
in-Furness was then included, when only 31 years
of age. The invitation was confirmed by the Conference of 1867. In six years he rose to a position
of influence which also devolved upon him weighty
responsibilities. He had serving under him two other
ministers and two accepted candidates from the
President's List of Reserve. His administration of
this large circuit (stretching along the coast from
Arnside, in Westmoreland, to Millom, in Cumberland, and embracing all the towns between) was
characterised by uncommon vigour, and followed by
encouraging success. Alexander the Great was in
India at 30, Napoleon in Italy at 26. In the arts
and letters amazing work has been achieved long
before middle life has been attained. Raphael, Burns,
Byron, Lucan, and Sir Isaac Newton attained to
fame in early manhood, and, strangest of all such
instances, Pitt in his twenty-first year became Prime
Minister of England ! These men were rare instances
of intellectual vigour and extraordinary genius. Mr.
Briscombe's first term of ministerial work, when
quite a young man, gave promise of great ability as
an administrator in the Methodist Church. It was
in this circuit that he was first brought into prominence as a popular controversialist. The Rev.
John Bilsborrow, Roman Catholic priest, then
resident at Barrow-in-Furness, now the Right Rev.

Mgr. Bilsborrow, Rector of St. Joseph's College, Upholland, Wigan, was delivering a series of lectures in his church disparaging Protestantism. Reports of these lectures were inserted each week in the *Barrow Herald*. Mr, Briscombe, seeing these distorted accounts of Protestantism, accompanied by an effort to disseminate the errors of the Roman Church, alike opposed to the true and Primitive Catholic Church as to Protestantism, began a series of lectures in reply. The Rev. John Bilsborrow's attack on Protestantism took the form of a series of lectures on Henry VIII., whom he assumed to be the founder of English Protestantism. In disparaging that monarch's character he sought with subtle skill to damage the Protestant religion by insinuating that he was the author of it, and that it sprang from his unbridled lusts. Mr. Briscombe, seeing that the truth of Protestantism was being misrepresented, came forth as its defender. This forcibly recalls the courage of Luther, as he drew near the door which was about to admit him into the presence of his judges (the Diet of Worms), when he met a valiant knight, the celebrated George, of Feundsberg. The old general, seeing Luther pass, tapped him on the shoulder, and, shaking his head blanched by many battles, said, "Thou art now going to make a nobler stand than I or any other captain ever made in the bloodiest of our battles; but if thy cause is just, and thou art sure of it, go forward in God's name and fear nothing, God will

not forsake thee." A noble tribute of respect paid
by the courage of the sword to the courage of the
mind.

INCIDENTS IN THE DISCUSSION WITH A ROMAN
CATHOLIC PRIEST.

Mr. Briscombe's first reply to these lectures was
given in the form of a sermon explaining the true
and only basis of the Protestant religion. It was
preached on Sunday evening, the 17th January,
1869. A full report appeared in the *Barrow Herald*,
Saturday, January 23rd, from which, as the best
means of setting forth the aim and spirit of the controversy, we extract the following condensed report :
" On Sunday evening last the Rev. Walter Briscombe preached in the Wesleyan Chapel, Hindpool-
road, on ' The word of God the sole authority in
matters of faith, and not the Church of Rome.' As
this was the first of a series of discourses to be given
in answer to the lectures of the Rev. J. Bilsborrow,
which are reported weekly in the *Barrow Herald*,
much interest was excited, and the spacious chapel
was entirely filled. The rev. gentleman took for his
text Acts xvii., 11, 12 : ' These were more noble
than those in Thessalonica, in that they received
the Word with all readiness of mind, and searched
the Scriptures daily, whether those things were so.
Therefore many of them believed.' This text (said
the preacher) contains the very pith and spirit of
the subject that has been announced for this evening's
discourse—' The Word of God the sole authority in

matters of faith, and not the Church of Rome.' As
you are aware, the sermon this evening is of a controversial character. Protestantism has been assailed;
and believing its principles and teachings to be true,
and holding all its doctrines to be Scriptural in their
character, it is incumbent upon us who are called
to proclaim the truth as it is in Jesus to rally round
and defend these everlasting truths. We prefer
peace and quietness, but the truth is assailed, and
as truth is dearer to us than quietness we do not
hesitate to undertake its vindication. I have read
all the sermons of the Rev. Mr. Bilsborrow that
have appeared in the *Barrow Herald*. For the
present suffice it to say that the lectures on Henry
the VIIIth furnish no argument against Protestantism, seeing that, according to the rev. gentleman's
own showing, that monarch was born in the Church
of Rome, lived in its faith, and wrote in support of
its doctrines. He also persecuted all his Protestants,
died in the belief of the Roman Creed, and made a
Roman Catholic will providing for masses to be said
for his soul. Protestants no more speak in commendation of Henry the VIIIth than does the rev.
lecturer. Protestant writers have never spoken in
commendation of the courses he pursued. On the
contrary their principles are antagonistic to his acts,
which were ruled by the dogmas of the Church of
Rome, in which belief it is known he both lived and
died. Henry the VIIIth was no more a Protestant
than Victor Emmanuel, King of Italy. Each king

retained the doctrines of the Church of Rome though both renounced the supremacy of the Pope. Again, if the arguments against the unchastity of Henry the VIIIth hold good, do they not equally apply to the unquestioned unchastity of Isabella, the present ex-Queen of Spain? Why should the Rev. Mr. Bilsborrow be so severe in condemning Henry the VIIIth, a believer in every Roman Catholic doctrine except the supremacy of the Pope, and yet pass by the same vices in a living Roman Catholic ex-monarch, to whom the Pope recently sent the golden rose, which he annually bestows upon the most pious monarch of Christendom?

"But, apart from the personal misconduct of noted men who took different sides at the Reformation, I will endeavour to prove that the first and greatest point of controversy—the Radical difference between the Church of Rome and the Protestant Church—is our subject for this evening : that ' The Word of God is the sole authority in matters of Faith.'

" The Roman Catholic Church denies this proposition and alleges her own authority to be final in matters of religious truth. POPE PIUS VII, in 1816, issued a bull to the Archbishop of Gnesin, Primate of Poland, in which he condemns the circulation of the Scriptures by Bible Societies as 'A crafty device by which the very foundations of religion are undermined, a pestilence which must be remedied and abolished, a defilement of the faith, eminently dangerous to souls.' LEO XII, in a bull to his clergy in Ireland in 1824 says : 'The Bible Society is dispreading itself through the whole world. After despising the traditions of the holy Fathers and in opposition to the well-known decree of the Council of Trent, this Society has collected all its forces and directs every means to one object—The translation, or rather the perversion of the Bible into the vernacular languages of all nations. From this fact there is strong ground of fear lest as in some instances already known, so likewise in the rest, through a perverted interpretation, there be framed out of the Gospel of Christ, a gospel of man, or, what is still worse, a gospel of the devil.' The numerous scholars who are capable of detecting any perversions of translation would not have been slow to do so had any existed. But the Roman Church might have circulated her own translation had she been willing to let the people have the word of God, and, indeed, the Bible Society has offered to sell her own translation in Roman Catholic communities if she would permit the people to read it. Hence, it is evident, she does not wish her people to read the Holy Scriptures even in translations made by Roman Catholic Divines.

"The Roman Church objects to private judgment in reading the Scriptures, yet she forgets that the Scriptures are always addressed to the private judgment of the readers. Nearly all the Epistles were addressed to the private members of the Church and not its ministers. Thus Paul addresses to the private members of the Church the following Epistles : ' To *all* that be in Rome, beloved of God,' ' Unto the Church of God, which is at Corinth, to them that are sanctified in Christ Jesus ;' ' Unto the Church of God which is in Corinth, with *all* the saints which are in all Asia (2nd Epistle) ;' ' To the churches of Galatia ;' ' To *all* the saints which are at Ephesus, and to the faithful in Christ Jesus ;' ' To *all* the saints at Philippi *with* the bishops and deacons;' ' To the saints and faithful brethren which are at Colosse ;' ' When this Epistle is read amongst you cause that it be read also in the Church of the Laodiceans, and that ye likewise read the Epistle from Laodicea,' &c. In writing a Pastoral Epistle to Timothy St. Paul declares that ' All Scripture— is profitable for doctrine, for reproof, for correction, for instruction in righteousness, that the man of God may be perfect and thoroughly furnished unto all good works.' Peter wrote ' to the strangers scattered throughout Pontus, Galatia, Cappadocia, Asia, and Bithynia ;' and ' to them that had obtained like precious faith.' St. John says to the private members of the Church : ' These things I write unto you that ye sin not,' and in the opening out of the book of Revelation he says to them : ' Blessed is he that readeth, and they that hear the words of this prophecy.' These citations form but a small portion of the passages of Scripture which require the private members of the Church to read for their instruction the Word of God.

"There is only one passage where there is the slightest semblance of a restriction in the reading of the Sacred Book, and that apparent restriction arises from an obscurity in the rendering. It occurs in 2 Peter, i, 20, and reads : 'Knowing this first, that no prophecy of the Scripture is of any private interpretation,' &c. 'Private interpretation' (*idias epiluseoos*) means of 'one's own unfolding,' having reference to the *prophet* not the *reader*. The meaning of St. Peter is expressed in the following rendering : 'No prophecy of the Scripture is of the prophet's own unfolding;' and this meaning is immediately confirmed by the statement which follows, that what the prophet wrote was *not his own private opinion*, but, *the unfolded Will of God* ; 'For (he adds) prophecy came not in old times by the will of man, but holy men of God spoke as they were moved by the Holy Ghost.' That this was St. Peter's meaning is also verified by the verse preceding this passage where the Apostle urges the private Christians in the churches to which he wrote, 'To take heed unto the sure word of prophecy as unto a light that shineth in a dark place.' It is incredible that he would *condemn* the private reading of the Word by believers in the very next sentence to that where he urgently *commends it !*

"Having considered what the sacred scriptures themselves teach on the obligation of private Christians to read them, we shall call attention to the evidence that *all* the Catholic Fathers of the Church, as opposed to the authority of the Roman Church, urged the duty of the private reading of the Word of God upon private Christians. The true Catholic Church in its earliest writings encouraged private Christians to read for themselves the Word of God. Protestantism is the staunch defender of this primitive Catholic teaching. It received its name from protesting against any additions to the Catholic Creed of the last Catholic Council of the Church, expressed in what is called the Nicene Creed. And, as the true defender of the Catholic Creed, it must ever protest against the doctrines which the Roman Church, alone, ventured to add to it at the Council of Trent. That the real Catholic Fathers of the Church encouraged the general reading of the Word of God, and regarded it as their highest standard of appeal, will appear from the following extracts from their works : Irenæus (A.D., 177) says : ' We have known the method of our salvation by no other than those by whom the Gospel came to us, which Gospel they then truly preached, but afterwards, by the Will of God, they delivered to us in the Scriptures to be, *for the future*, the foundation and pillar of our faith !' 'Read more diligently that Gospel which is given us by the Apostles, and read more diligently the prophets, and you will find every action and *the whole doctrine of the Lord* preached in them.' Again, alluding to heretics, he says : ' For when they are accused by Scripture they turn upon the accusation of Scripture itself, as though it were not entirely correct or of authority.' So did Irenaeus encourage the reading of Scripture and uphold it as the greatest Christian authority. Tertullian (A.D., 200) writes : ' If I find no *written law* for the thing, it follows that tradition hath sanctioned by usage this custom which by a rational interpretation must possess apostolic authority.' This early Christian writer thus distinctly recognises the *authority* of ' all written law ' above any ecclesiastical traditions. Clement of Alexandria (A.D., 200) says : ' Scripture we use for the finding out of things ; this we use as the *rule of judging.*' 'They that are ready to spend their time in the best things, will not give over seeking truth until they have found the *demonstrations from the Scriptures* themselves.' ' They must expound Scriptures by Scriptures, and by the analogy of faith, comparing spiritual things with spiritual, one place with another, and all by the proportion to the Divine attributes.' Origen (A.D., 200) writes : ' If anything yet remain which the Holy Scripture doth not determine, no other third Scripture (*i. e.*, none other after the Old and New Testaments) ought to be received for authorising any knowledge or doctrine.' ' It is necessary for us to call the Scriptures into testimony, for our meanings and narrations, without those witnesses, have no claim to belief.' ' No man ought, for the confirmation of doctrines, to use books which are not canonized Scriptures.' · How imminent is their danger who neglect to study the Scriptures, in which alone a knowledge of their condition can be ascertained.' Cyprian (A.D., 250) challenging the worth of a mere tradition which had been alleged by a fellow bishop, says : ' Doth it descend from the Lord's authority, or from the commands and epistles of the Apostles ? For those things are to be done which are written therein. If it be commanded in the Gospels, or the epistles and Acts of the Apostles, then let the holy tradition be observed.' In this expostulation he clearly places the authority of Scripture far above all tradition, and makes it the test of credible tradition. Hippolytus (A.D., 230) writes : ' Whosoever of us will exercise piety towards God, *cannot learn this but out of the Holy Scriptures.* Whatsoever therefore the Holy Scriptures proclaim, that let us know, and whatsoever they teach that let us understand.' Athanasius (A.D., 340) writes : ' The Holy Scriptures, given by the inspiration of God, *are of themselves sufficient toward the discovery of truth.*' ' The *Catholic Christians* (says he) will neither speak nor endure to hear anything in religion that is foreign to Scripture.' 'The Protestants are, for this reason the true ' Catholic Christians,' because, like the ' Catholic Christians ' of the first four centuries of Christianity, in matters of Christian faith they will neither speak nor endure to hear anything in religion that is foreign to Scripture.' Cyril (A.D., 360) says : ' Not even the least of the divine and holy mysteries of the faith ought to be handed down without the Divine Scriptures. Do not simply give faith to me while I am speaking these things to you, *except you have the proof of what I say from the Holy Word.* For the security and *preservation* of our faith are not sustained by ingenuity of speech, but by the proofs of what I say from the Holy Word.' Chrysostom (A.D., 400) writes: 'The Scripture, like a safe door, *doth prevent an entrance to heretics, guiding us in safety in all things and not permitting us to be deceived.*' 'Formerly, it might have been ascertained by various means which was the true Church, but, at present, *there is no other method left for those who are willing to discover the true Church, but by the Scriptures alone.*' The Sainted Chrysostom, the greatest bishop of the 4th century, thus lays down in other, but equally clear words, that "The Word of God is the sole authority in matters of faith.' Theophilus (A.D., 412) says: 'It is the part of a devilish spirit to think anything to be divine that is not in the authority of Holy Scripture.' Jerome, who belonged to the Roman Church, and was one of its most eminent scholars in the 4th century, says: 'Those things made and found, as it were by Apostolic tradition, *without the authority and testimony of Scripture,* the Word of God smites.' 'That which hath no authority from Scripture is with equal facility despised as it is proved.' Augustine, in the 4th century, who also was one of the most brilliant saints and writers of the Roman Church, writes: 'In those matters which are clearly laid down in Scripture, *all things*

may be found which pertain to faith and morals.'
' All writings since the confirmation of the Canon
of Scripture are liable to dispute, and even Councils
themselves are to be examined and amended by
Councils.' ' I am unwilling that the Church should
be demonstrated by human documents, but by Divine
Oracles.'

"It was this recognition of the Supremacy of the
Holy Scriptures above the authority of alleged traditions and actual Councils that Augustine contended.
He believed and advocated this view on the ground
that it was taught clearly and consistently in the
Word of God, and that all the Catholic Fathers of the
Primitive Church taught it as clearly and consistently.
The quotations from the early Fathers of the Church
might be largely multiplied, but those selected
showed that Protestant Christianity was fulfilling
the truest Biblical and noblest Catholic mission in
protesting against any additions, either by the
Roman Church or any other churches, to the doctrines
of the real Catholic faith, or to the final authority in
all matters of religion.

" Such, said the rev. gentleman, in conclusion,
were the reasons he had endeavoured to place before
them that evening in vindication of the Protestant
churches. Whatever difference there might be in
minor matters, all Protestants are agreed upon the
sufficiency of the Word of God as the sole rule of
faith. Here is our Unity—a unity in the recognition of one and the same standard of faith and

morals, allowing liberty of forms in working out the self-same principles. We turn to the Scriptures alone as our final court of appeal, as did the Primitive Catholic Church. If Protestantism is antagonistic to the Word of God, God grant that it may be stamped out of existence, but if accordant therewith, may God cause it increasingly to prevail! We, like the Bereans commended in my text, will ' Search the Scriptures daily whether these things be so.' God grant that we may more earnestly love that Word, more firmly believe its doctrines, more fully obey its precepts, and, at length, all attain that eternal bliss it so gloriously describes! The rev. lecturer concluded by announcing that next Sunday evening his discourse will be on ' The Disunity of the Church of Rome.' "

We have given the substance of this first controversial sermon in a large degree, but not to its full extent. It may be regarded both in its tone of speech, manner of treatment, and its argumentative style, as a fair specimen of his part in the long controversy which followed. It extended over seven weeks in the pulpit and the press, at the end of which time the Rev. Mr. Bilsborrow suddenly fell ill. As soon as Mr. Briscombe heard of his illness he recalled from the press a controversial letter he had already sent, and in its place wrote the following letter, which appeared in the *Barrow Herald* of Feb. 27th, 1869 :—

"*To the Editor of the Barrow Herald.*

" Sir,—I have previously sent a letter to you on the controversy between the Rev. Mr. Bilsborrow and myself, requesting its insertion in your next issue, but having heard that the rev. gentleman is ill, I beg to request that you will not insert it. I should be very sorry to put the rev. gentleman to the excitement of controversy in his present state, and would add that, though I differ from him in doctrine, I respect his sincere attachment to the Church of his choice, and fervently pray that Divine grace may console him in his affliction, and vouchsafe to him a speedy restoration.

" Yours truly,

" W. BRISCOMBE."

In this manner Mr. Briscombe's first public controversy was brought to a close. The Roman Catholic priest happily recovered from his illness, and soon began to resume his public duties. Another year revolved round, in the course of which the Vatican Council of the Church of Rome was convoked, and added several new doctrines to the Creed of that Church. The Rev. Mr. Bilsborrow began a series of lectures on the subject of the Council, with the apparent intention of preparing his people to receive its decrees. These lectures, being reported in the press, were replied to by the Rev. Mr. Briscombe, and a second controversy of considerable length immediately ensued. The topics were different, but still bore on the chief points of distinction between the Protestant and Roman Catholic Churches. This controversy in the press and pulpit lasted for nearly three months. It was conducted much in the same spirit and style by the disputants as the preceding one. Towards the close of the controversy, the Rev. J. M. Crolly, Roman Catholic priest, of Millom, began to contribute to the controversy by giving a series of lectures on the same subjects. He secured the insertion of several in the *Barrow Herald*, but sundry writers called the attention of the editor to the fact of the unfairness of his being allowed to aid the disputation on that side, and that supplementary contingent was set aside. It is just to report that, though in such controversies parties are commonly in favour of their own sides, Mr. Briscombe, while presenting strong arguments, treated his opponent with perfect courtesy, and it was the general impression that the effect of the controversy was greatly to confirm the belief of Protestant truth without leaving in the town a sting of personal bitterness.

THE ROCHDALE CIRCUIT.

On finishing his three years ministry in the Ulverston Circuit, Mr. Briscombe, having previously accepted an invitation to the Rochdale Wesley Circuit, was duly appointed by the Conference of 1870, and in the month of September began his labours there. Being second minister here, he felt a great relief from the many and more responsible duties of administering a wide and newly developing circuit.

Into the ordinary duties of a circuit minister he threw a large amount of energy, and was highly appreciated both as a pastor and preacher. Mr. Briscombe, in addition to the general duties of the circuit, conducted a Young Men's Improvement Class, and Mrs. Briscombe a Young Women's Bible Class, both of which were specially successful in attaching the members of the classes to the Church, and in promoting an elevated and carefully regulated intercourse among the young men and young women. On sundry occasions, especially of a festive kind, the two classes were accustomed to meet together. On leaving the circuit at the expiration of three years, among many tokens of good-will from friends in general, each of the classes presented to its leader a handsomely framed photograph of the members and leader, mementoes which have often recalled the pleasure of the pleasant and useful association.

A Continental Holiday, and how it was utilised.

Mr. Briscombe finished his ministerial labours in Rochdale three weeks before the ordinary time, in order to take a holiday in the interval of changing circuits. He and Mrs. Briscombe had previously accepted a cordial invitation to visit Mr. and Mrs. Leonard Kayberry, two highly esteemed friends, then resident in Ghent, though previously living in Rochdale. It is not needful to record the common incidents of a tour to Belgium, but an unexpected opportunity of usefulness occurred which may prove of some interest to the reader, and shew the possibilities of usefulness in taking a holiday. Mr. and Mrs. Kayberry were very intelligent and warmhearted Methodists, and keenly felt the loss of their religious privileges in a great city of 150,000 people, almost all Roman Catholics. There were only two small Protestant Churches in the city, and their services were conducted in Flemish, French being chiefly spoken by the upper classes. On account of language they could not profit in these native Protestant services. There was only one service in the English, on a Sunday, conducted by a chaplain of the Church of England. The chaplain was not at all acceptable to the English residents, and really lived at Brussels, limiting his visits to Ghent to the hurried conducting of this one service. It was said he surrendered himself to the continental laxity of observing the Lord's Day. The effect was an average congregation of about 12, except when increased by English visitors. Mr. Kayberry secured the loan of one of the Flemish churches for two Sunday evenings, and Mr. Briscombe preached on both occasions. The English residents were duly informed through the press and post, and about 100 assembled each evening. The first Sunday evening, when Mr. Briscombe was praying with great animation, he heard a quiet commotion, and at the close of the prayer, on opening his eyes, he saw the two aisles of the church almost filled with working men in their *sabots* and blue blouses, standing and gazing in wonder at himself. As soon as he began to read the lesson they quietly withdrew. It was supposed it was the fervid, extemporaneous, and foreigh prayer that had attracted their attention when passing the church doors. Prayers being there generally read and more tamely expressed, rendered the fervent and spontaneous prayer of a Methodist minister a marvel to the simple mirded Flemings. These services were so highly appreciated that Mr. Kayberry desired Mr. Briscombe to use his best efforts to secure the sending of a Methodist minister to open a mission for the resident English in Ghent. On his return he had an interview with the late Rev. Luke H. Wiseman, M.A., cn the subject, judging that his great influence at the mission house might compass this end. Mr. Wiseman appeared deeply interested in the question, and desired further information. His lamented decease occurred soon after, which interrupted the consideration of the subject. Not long after, Mr. Briscombe received information that the people had undertaken the matter themselves. They had heard of a devout Presbyterian minister at Brussels, 40 miles distant, who had a small English Protestant charge there, and whose Sunday evenings were free from public duty. They elected a deputation to interview him, and, if possible, secure his services for each Sunday evening. They happily succeeded, as train service suited the arrangement. He always stayed over till Monday, and on that evening conducted a Bible class for his little flock. He also administered to them at stated times the sacred ordinance of the Lord's Supper. Several years after, Mr. Briscombe heard that this mission was still successfully going on. The return of Mr. and Mrs. Kayberry to England broke off his communication, and since that period he has only heard about the cause once ; but that information was of a very favourable kind, and was given him by one of the English families which had returned from Ghent to the neighbourhood of Bury.

THE RAWTENSTALL CIRCUIT.

Having accepted an invitation to the neighbouring circuit of Rawtenstall, Mr. and Mrs. Briscombe duly removed thither after the Conference of 1873. Still serving as second minister he found ample opportunity for pastoral work in a circuit somewhat limited in area, and fair scope for special work amongst the young men and Sunday school teachers. He was president of a successful Young Men's Class at Rawtenstall, and of a still more successful one at Crawshawbooth, the second place in the circuit. The former class was organised during his residence at Rawtenstall, but the latter class was a successful institution of long standing. It owed its permanence and a great measure of its success to several resident gentlemen who acted as vice-presidents, of whom, perhaps, the most notable was the late Dr. Kerr. Mr. Briscombe also conducted a very successful Bible Class for Sunday school teachers at Newchurch, in the same circuit. In most respects his ministry in the Rawtenstall Circuit followed the same lines, and had an equal measure of acceptability as in the preceding Rochdale Circuit.

BARROW-IN-FURNESS CIRCUIT.

This new and rising town having been separated from the Ulverston Circuit and constituted a new one in 1872, Mr. Briscombe, almost three years beforehand, was invited to become its superintendent. At the expiration of his three years term at Rawtenstall, in the year 1876, he removed to Barrow-in-Furness. Soon after he had accepted the invitation this important new centre of population had received a great check to its trade. Commercial depression set in on a large scale, and by the time that he had settled in the town there was a large amount of poverty amongst the working classes, many of them being unable to find employment. He soon connected himself with efforts to relieve the suffering poor, both amongst his own people and those unattached to his own church, and contributed a considerable amount of influence to the benevolent work by stimulating others to co-operate in the enterprise.

The commercial depression of the town added seriously to the financial difficulties of working the circuit, and these financial difficulties were seriously aggravated by schemes of chapel building begun when trade was very prosperous. What added more to the difficulties of this situation was that the three small school-chapels which had been undertaken at such a crisis were involved in debt beyond their actual value. In addition to all the ordinary expenses of providing for the circuit, £200 was required each year to pay the interest on moneys borrowed for these new erections. To make the matter still worse all the circuit was contained in the borough of Barrow-in-Furness, so that there were no outside places of a prosperous kind to aid the temporary distress of the town, and, what was perhaps worst of all, the congregations at the new places were very slender, so that all these probably unequalled circuit financial responsibilities devolved mainly on the society and congregation of the old chapel at Hindpool-road.

Mr. Briscombe, having exercised the superintendency over Barrow-in-Furness six years before, when it was in the Ulverston Circuit, was well known, and enjoyed the strongest confidence of his people. With this he was stimulated in entering on his work, and, being well supported by his people, he was enabled to rise above difficulties which a Conference Commission, that had sat on the case, pronounced to be the most serious of the kind in the Connexion.

THE CHRISTADELPHIAN CONTROVERSY.

Mr. Briscombe had not been long in Barrow before circumstances called him into another important and prolonged controversy. Like Nehemiah, he carried both sword and trowel in fulfilling his mission, and in addition to building up his people in the truth he defended them also against the insidious advocacy of serious errors. The immediate occasion of the controversy was an advertisement inserted in the *Barrow Herald* for many weeks, which, in order to suggest that man's immortality was not taught in the Bible, professed to offer

£100 CHALLENGE TO PROVE MAN'S IMMORTALITY FROM THE SCRIPTURES.

Apparently during Mr. Briscombe's six years absence from Barrow a new sect calling themselves Christadelphians had entered the town, and were endeavouring to establish their cause. They were largely availing themselves of the press by public advertisements and challenges to spread their peculiar doctrines. The following advertisement appeared in the *Barrow Herald*, October, 1876, for several weeks :

"£100 REWARD.—The above reward will be given to any person who can produce a text of Scripture which states that man is possessed of an immortal or never-dying soul. The attention of those who burn Christadelphian tracts is especially called to this announcement. Anyone claiming the reward is requested to apply at the Christadelphian Synagogue, Cavendish-street, any Tuesday evening from eight to nine o'clock."

To this advertisement Mr. Briscombe spiritedly replied by a letter to the paper, in which it appeared as follows :—

"*To the Editor of the Barrow Herald.*

"Sir,—I observed in your issue of Saturday last that a community of religious people, designating themselves Christadelphians, have offered £100 prize to anyone proving from Scripture 'that man is possessed of an immortal or never-dying soul.' I desire to inform them, through the medium of your paper, by which they have made known their offer, that if they will deposit the amount in the hands of the mayor, or other person of position in the borough, as a proof of their sincerity in the offer, I will endeavour to prove from Holy Scripture that man is possessed of an immortal spirit. The arguments may be submitted to a select number of gentlemen accustomed to sift evidence, such as magistrates and members of the legal profession, or to a public meeting, which should decide by a majority of votes whether or not in their opinion the evidence presented would entitle me to the prize. In the event of securing the award I would pledge myself to give it all to local charities.

" I am, truly yours,

" WALTER BRISCOMBE.

" 16, Storey-square, October 18th, 1876."

Several letters were written urging the Christadelphians to deposit the award offered, and to discuss the doctrine of man's inherent immortality, which they so emphatically deny in all their publications, and which they plainly denied in their advertisement. All, however, were unavailing, so the discussion in that form never came off. The following week their challenge was withdrawn from the press. These incidents having aroused the interest and curiosity of many people, Mr. Briscombe was desired to give some lectures on the subject, to which he responded by delivering one, in the first instance, on "The Contradictions of Annihilationism," in the Hindpool-road Wesleyan Chapel, in 1876. The lecture was a very able and successful assault on their theory of man's annihilation, showing that it was in direct conflict with the admitted doctrines of the resurrection and judgment. This lecture is contained in the book named in the footnote A. No sooner had it been given than the Christadelphians brought one of their chief men from London under the name of

ANTIPAS, F.D.,

to reply to it. He delivered his lecture in the Town Hall, and at its close challenged Mr. Briscombe to a discussion. The challenge of Antipas was like the folly of the man who professed to have studied the question of the earth's sphericity, and having arrived at the conclusion that it was not a sphere at all, but an immense plane, challenged all the philosophers of England to prove the contrary. Mr. Briscombe, unknown to the lecturer, was at the opposite end of the large and crowded hall, and upon hearing the challenge rose to his feet and moved towards the platform. His advance to the platform was the signal for a loud outburst of cheering. He first asked the lecturer for a definition of the two words, "annihilation" and "resurrection," in both of which doctrines the

---

A. "Hades, Heaven, and Gehenna (or Hell)." By the Rev. Walter Briscombe.

lecturer had avowed his belief. His replies were at first evasive, which the meeting recognising broke out into a storm of indignation at his course. Mr. Briscombe, having already shown that the Christadelphians taught that annihilation denoted extinction of personality, and that resurrection denoted the reproduction of the same person, held that as annihilation reduced a person to a state of non-existence, a person brought from a state of non-existence into actual being was not a resurrection but an act of creation. Upon asking the lecturer to explain how an annihilated man could undergo a resurrection, and how, when existence had once been extinguished, it could have the continuity necessary to personal identity and judgment, Antipas replied, "I shall not answer Mr. Briscombe's query, but will bid you all good night," retiring, as he said it, by a side door from the platform amid a vociferous storm of hisses. The result of the short discussion was of such a character as to lead the *Barrow Herald* to head the report of the meeting by the brief expression—

"ANTIPAS DISCOMFITED."

The newspaper reports of the sudden collapse of this important discussion brought into the controversy Mr. Kellaway, a London publisher, a believer in annihilation, though not a Christadelphian. He threw down the gauntlet in a letter to the *Barrow Herald*, in which he besought Mr. Briscombe "for God's sake, for Christ's, for the truth's, and for humanity's sake, to debate the subject with him."

With other equally vehement appeals he pressed the matter, alleging as his reason for the urgency that Mr. Briscombe "had carried things with so high a hand." The sense in which Mr. Kellaway meant the last phrase may be inferred from another of his letters that shortly followed, in which he refers to a complaint of "Antipas" against him. "If Antipas," says he, "wants to know how I came to have any-thing to say to Mr. Briscombe, I must needs acquaint him with the *unpleasant fact* that one of his own number wrote me a pressing letter to come to the rescue," &c.—*Barrow Herald*, February 3rd, 1877. This beseeching pathetic challenge brought Mr. Briscombe again into the arena of controversy in defence of biblical doctrines. The debate was con-tinued for about three months in the columns of the *Barrow Herald*. Mr. Kellaway throughout this con-troversy sought to avert the force of Mr. Briscombe's arguments by bending and twisting facts to suit his theory, and attaching other significations to the words " annihilation," " self-identity," and " resurrection.'' These words being of essential importance to the argument of the matter in dispute, Mr. Briscombe insisted on having them defined and used in a fixed sense. It is said that once on a time a novice in science, with the aid of a powerful telescope, thought he had discovered a living monster in the sun. He calculated its dimensions, speculated upon its habitudes, and satisfied himself that it must ere long devour the solar orb, and then our world would be ruined. He gathered some scientific friends about him, informed them of the frightful fact, and begged them to investigate it for themselves. They looked, and saw the horrid creature apparently gnawing his way into the very centre of the sun! At last one of the company, more curious and more sceptical than the rest, suggested an examination of the instrument, when lo! a fly was found enclosed between the glasses. So it was seen and acknowledged as the discussion proceeded that Mr. Kellaway's vision of the subject had been distorted through the lens of his imagination by the huge prejudice which had intercepted his view and he wisely withdrew from the controversy; but Mr. Briscombe continued his arguments until he had (as was the general impression) completely shattered the Christadelphian theory of annihilation. A friend who knew Mr. Briscombe, when located in Barrow, but was not of his Creed, has told the writer that he never knew an orthodox Dissenting minister more free from religious bigotry and intolerance. Mr. Briscombe, he said, was never uncharitable to anyone, whatever his belief, and never spoke harshly or discourteously of the persons with whom he engaged in controversy, however much he felt bound to oppose their sentiments.

Mr. Briscombe, whilst manifesting unfailing courtesy to his opponents, did not shrink from presenting strong arguments. The Rev. Andrew Fuller was right when he said, "I should suspect that a man's preaching had but little salt in it if no galled horse did wince." Mr. Briscombe's religious and public services in Barrow during these three years were greatly valued ; and in circuit administration, preaching, and pastorising, he gave the very highest satisfaction to his people. The heavy debts were largely liquidated, the circuit income kept well up, his stipend was advanced £20 per year, the congregations increased, and the membership was well maintained, despite a decrease of many thousands of inhabitants during the period of commercial depression, for it was not till the end of his term of service that the trade of the town began to revive. His last service before leaving the circuit was somewhat remarkable as an expression of popular esteem. The Chapel Stewards, foreseeing that the chapel would be far too small for the congregation, secured the Town Hall. The spacious building was, however, filled half-an-hour before the time, and many hundreds were unable to gain admission. In addition to many tokens of kindness received from friends a subscription was raised to defray the expenses of a visit to Switzerland, which gave him a much needed holiday after three years of incessant toil amongst a people who warmly supported his various enterprises, held him in high esteem, and greatly admired his abilities as a minister of the Gospel of Christ.

CATHCART ROAD CIRCUIT, GLASGOW.

Having accepted an invitation to Cathcart Circuit some length of time before his term ended at

Barrow, he was duly appointed there by the Conference of 1879, and proceeded thither at the customary time of changing Circuits. Methodism in Scotland, though true in all essential points to the Methodism of England, is somewhat modified in non-essential points by the influence of the Presbyterian Church, which includes the great bulk of the Scotch people. The chief matter in which Scotch Methodism differs from the English Methodist customs is in the greater concentration of ministerial labours. The Circuits are smaller, and the minister, though limited, as in England, to a three years ministry, has, for that short time, a much better opportunity of converging his activities, so as to intensify the personal influence of his ministry. This was Mr. Briscombe's ideal of the most suitable method of giving a Methodist minister the best chances for accomplishing, by personal influence, the greatest good of his charge.

CHAPEL TOO BIG.

On entering upon his work he found a chapel seating about 450 people moderately well attended, but capable of holding a very much larger congregation. After being there about six weeks, he commenced a series of special discourses on the "Future Life," which continued for ten Sunday evenings in succession. He succeeded against great odds, and in face of difficulties, in laying his hand on a large number of young people in the city. Soon the congregation became a sight to make one glad. Grave and reverend seniors were seen here and there ;

while young men abounded sitting everywhere, the aisles of the chapel being filled. Even on that memorable night, the last Sunday in 1879, in which the Tay Bridge was blown down by the terrible hurricane which raged for hours and caused such great destruction to life and property, the chapel was crowded in every part eager to hear the last of the series. Mr. Briscombe made his ministry so attractive that the ordinary congregation was largely increased, which immediately manifested itself in an augumented offertory. From that time the weekly offerings were permauently doubled, which was maintained throughout the three years, adding very largely to the financial prosperity of the circuit. The circuit spontaneously recognised its appreciation of this success by raising his stipend from £180 to £200 the year following, and paying that amount retrospectively from the commencement of his ministry among them.

CHAPEL TOO LITTLE.

In about six months after the commencement of his ministry there, all the unoccupied pews were taken and more were enquired for. It was suggested at one of the official meetings that there should be a scheme of enlargement undertaken. It was said by some that the large congregations would only be temporary, and afterwards revert to their ordinary size ; others said that the smallest possible outlay for enlargement would cost £400, and that it would be too great an effort for the small Church to raise it, which had to support its own minister entirely, in addition to all the other claims that devolved upon the circuit. The matter fell into abeyance for another six months, when one of the leading officials, gathering confidence from the progress of the congregations, said, in his opinion, the question of enlargement should be looked at. This led to steps being taken to consider the matter. At the first trustees' meeting called for the purpose of considering the enlargement, it was again calculated that the least possible outlay would cost £400, and that this sum would be too formidable to undertake till the way could be seen to raise it. Mr. Briscombe suggested that a number of gentlemen should be appointed to canvass the congregation before any direct steps were taken. This was agreed to, and the gentlemen were appointed for the work. On their meeting, at the time fixed after the canvass, by a remarkable coincidence, yet not the less providentially over-ruled, the sums promised amounted to precisely £400. This so encouraged the trustees that they resolved on a scheme of £800 at once. Subsequent meetings encouraged them to a still larger plan by adding to their project the erection of a new Sunday School to accommodate 400 children. In the course of eighteen months both

CHAPEL ENLARGEMENT AND SCHOOL ERECTION

were completed, at a cost of about £2,400. The trustees asked Mr. Briscombe to preach the first of the re-opening sermons, when a collection of £25 was taken, by far the largest amount taken at any of the after services. The New Chapel soon gained a congregation that regularly filled it, and the School received a considerable augmentation of scholars. The extension and erection, which had been very carefully and minutely studied, and watched over by the trustees, gave great satisfaction as being well adapted to the needs of the place. The raising of the money was attended with very little difficulty, and never caused any embarrassment, the whole of the debt being liquidated in a few years after the opening. It is just to add that the advance then made has not receded, but has on the contrary led to higher successes, maintained to the present day. After exercising his ministry six months under these new and improved conditions, by the rigid law of itinerancy he was under the necessity of removing to another sphere of labour. On his leaving, the Circuit Board voted to him a sum of money from the surplus income (which before his coming did not meet the circuit expenses) as an expression of the value they attached to his services.

Some time before his term of service ended, he had accepted an invitation to become the superintendent of the Irwell-street Circuit, Manchester. Shortly after making this engagement, he was waited upon by the Circuit Stewards of the newly-erected St. John's Methodist Church, Glasgow, to become its minister. This invitation, chiefly on the ground of its affording greater concentration of labour, was far more congenial to his inclination, and would have involved a higher stipend, but a sense of honour constrained him to abide true to his engagement with Irwell-street Circuit, Manchester.

Mr. Briscombe again Challenged to a Public Discussion.

During the time that Mr. Briscombe was at Glasgow the Rev. T. D. Anderson, B.A., wrote to him from Mumbles, a sea-side resort near Swansea, stating that a retired medical gentleman there had procured a pamphlet of Mr. Briscombe's on "The Contradictions of Annihilationism." The Christadelphians in that district were then busy unsettling the faith of Christian people by lectures, sermons, and tracts, and he thought that if Mr. Briscombe could be secured to deliver a few lectures on the subjects in controversy it would tend to allay the doubts of the people. Though not connected with the Methodist Church, but belonging to the Plymouth Brethren, he offered to defray all the expenses. Mr. Briscombe consented to deliver two sermons on the Sunday and four lectures the ensuing week bearing on the controverted points. The Sunday services were largely attended, and also the lectures that followed. Dr. Rawlings, of Swansea, presided on one occasion, the Chairman of the district on another, and two local gentlemen on the other evenings. A short time before these lectures were arranged for, a challenge to meet Mr. D. Roberts, of Birmingham, the leading writer and leader among the Christadelphians, was

sent to Mr. Briscombe. Mr. Briscombe accepted the
offer to discuss all the subjects with him in public at
Mumbles. Whilst the matter was being arranged
to come off in this form, Mr. Roberts, who had
accepted the offer to meet in debate at Mumbles at
the time of Mr. Briscombe's visit, wrote to ask for a
delay on account of a visit he wished to make to
Scotland. As Mr. Briscombe could not alter the
time agreed upon, the debate in that form never came
off, but he allowed the Christadelphians to ask any
questions they pleased at the end of each lecture, or
to state any difficulties that they could allege against
his arguments. This permission was largely used,
and if the pronouncement of a public audience,
especially of the thoughtful and orderly kind assembled on those occasions, may be regarded as a trust-
worthy verdict, he commanded, with the exception
of a few zealous Christadelphians, the general and
enthusiastic support of his audience. The thoughtful and popular mind appeared to be fully satisfied
with the issue, and so strong was the desire to have
his lectures in print, that, to overcome Mr. Briscombe's reluctance, they instantly subscribed £12 as
a guarantee against any loss in the publication. Mr.
Briscombe hitherto had only published one pamphlet,
and now, through the constraint of friends, he promised to publish all his lectures on a Future Life,
which he eventually did under the title of "Hades,
Heaven, and Gehenna (or Hell)." Mr. Briscombe
limited the first edition to private sale, and so the

book was not brought before the public with that prominence which, in all likelihood, would have assured it a much more extended sale. He published it when at Pendleton, and it was probably one of the contributory causes which tended to overtax his energies and lay him aside. In consequence of the failure of his health soon after, he kept all his books stored up, with the exception of the local calls for them in the places where the lectures had previously been delivered. His own diffidence in pushing the book has no doubt retarded the sale, for its merits as a storehouse of evidence on the subject, together with its remarkable harmonising of apparently conflicting views, and presentation of original thoughts on the subject, entitle it to a popularity far beyond the edition of a second thousand which it has now reached. We propose to give some extracts from it at the close of our sketch.

TYPHOID FEVER.

Just as he was finishing his three years' ministry in the Cathcart-road Circuit, he was seized with an attack of typhoid fever, the first serious illness of his life-time. He felt the incipient signs on the very last Sunday that brought his ministry to a close, in a violent head-ache, and a sense of bodily languor, but did not suspect the nature of the ailment. The next few days witnessed a rapid enfeeblement, when a lady and gentleman connected with his own Church, seeing his debility and the turmoil of the house in packing up for removal, invited himself, wife, and children (his little boy being then also very ill) to go and stay for a period at their house in a beautiful suburb called Cathcart. This invitation was accepted, and the transit made with suitable care. The doctor soon after was called in, who pronounced it a case of typhoid fever. This announcement created some measure of alarm, both to Mrs. Briscombe and himself. It was felt that it was a serious matter to have come to a friend's house under such circumstances. When the nature of his disease was made known to Mr. and Mrs. Scrimgeour, who were entertaining them, they at once relieved their anxiety by replying—"You could not be at a better house under the circumstances, as there are no other children here but yours, and we are very glad to be able to render this service." Mr. Briscombe, when relating this touching incident, said, with eyes filled with tears of gratitude, that the kindness and generosity of Mr. and Mrs. Scrimgeour cannot be overstated. Mr. Briscombe believes that, under the providence of God, he owes his restoration and prolonged life to the service they then rendered. There had been many cases of typhoid fever in the neighbourhood where Mr. Briscombe had lived, and the drain from his house was not properly trapped, as was found out when the matter was examined, though no one suspected it before. His continuance in the house under these circumstances would, according to all probability, have militated against his recovery, if indeed it had not rendered it impossible. Mr.

Briscombe always delights in recording that the service of Mr. and Mrs. Scrimgeour, on this occasion, was the most valuable and generous act of kindness he had ever the honour of receiving. He stayed with them about six weeks, by which time his health was sufficiently improved to travel to the home of his brother-in-law, Dr. Dyson, of Sheffield, where he remained a few weeks before going to his new circuit.

During his affliction, he realised under the influence of his religious principles great tranquillity of mind, which was doubtless favourable to his recovery. He asked for the prayers of his people, a request which indeed was by them anticipated, and he devoutly recognised the influence of prayer, as resulting in the providential arrangement which moved Mr. and Mrs. Scrimgeour to invite him to their home, which sustained him under his affliction, and which, by God's blessing, issued in his recovery.

THE IRWELL STREET CIRCUIT, MANCHESTER.

Mr. Briscombe's invitation to become the superintendent of this circuit, having been ratified by the appointment of conference, became the next sphere of his ministry. On account of the illness referred to, he was not able to begin his duties till the latter part of October. Even then he had not fully recovered his vigour, but his concern for his work prevailed over his weakness and over the contrary counsel of many of his friends, and he resumed duty in the hope that he would gradually grow stronger in its discharge. Probably he would have done so had not the special needs of the circuit placed a heavy strain upon him, and had not his own zeal outstripped his discretion. Fresh from a circuit where his preaching on special subjects had made such a successful impression, he attempted to work on the same lines. He began the same series of sermons on "The Future Life" which he first delivered as a series in his previous circuit. They again drew very large audiences, but, as on account of the more frequent pulpit changes, the ten discourses on the subject would have spread over a half year, he condensed them into half the number to compass them in a less space of time. One result was that the sermons became much longer, to crowd in the matter, and as he then preached with considerable vigour, his heart being yet weak from the effects of the fever, it told seriously upon his health. He was on many occasions attacked with alarming prostrations after some of these special efforts, so as to render him speechless and incapable of movement on account of extreme debility.

To add to the difficulty of the situation, the administration of the circuit required more than ordinary effort to meet its exigencies. A large and handsome Gothic chapel had been built at Pendleton, where he resided, and opened about a year before he entered on his duties as superintendent. It had cost about £14,000, and one half of that amount remained as debt, which needed to be considerably liquidated before the grants promised by the Chapel Committee could be secured. This formidable task, together with sundry difficulties of less importance, made necessary demands upon his enfeebled energies, which, with his ardent desire to surmount, at length prostrated him so frequently that, though he had received and accepted a cordial invitation at the March quarter to remain another year, he requested the ensuing Conference, by the advice of many friends, to allow him a year's rest from duty. This request was duly granted, and the next twelve months were spent in almost total rest from public speaking and preaching. For seven months he lived at Arnside in a ready furnished house placed at his disposal by an old friend in the Barrow Circuit—F. J. Crossfield, Esq. During the winter he conducted a bible class, which was well attended and highly appreciated. He also prepared, though he never published, a "Harmony of the Four Gospels." The remaining part of the year he spent at St. Annes-on-the-Sea, now and then taking a public service to test his returning strength, as indeed he had done occasionally at Arnside in a small Chapel.

THE CRANMER CIRCUIT, LIVERPOOL.

Mr. Briscombe's health having improved during his year's rest, he received a call from the Cranmer Circuit, Liverpool, to become the second minister, at the Conference following. As this relieved him from the responsibilities of superintendency and called him to a sphere of lighter labour than his last circuit, he favourably responded to it, and was duly appointed. His vigour was not fully restored when he again entered on his duties, but the circuit was indulgent, and the counsel of his medical adviser was that if he never overtaxed his energies, during the three years he spent at Bootle he would gradually recover his strength, and would become equal to all the duties of his calling. The death of the highly esteemed superintendant of the circuit—the Rev. Henry Pollinger—occurred during Mr. Briscombe's first year. He being the second minister, the superintendency then devolved upon him. The circuit was not strained by any special difficulties, therefore the extra demands upon him did not overtax his energies.

SHIPPING DEPRESSION.

Perhaps the most special event of his ministry at Bootle lay outside his proper circuit work, and was a somewhat uncommon exercise of social benevolence, at least in point of degree. Those who are familiar with Liverpool and its surroundings cannot fail being impressed with its great luxury and poverty, the evidences of wealth and of squalor which follow so closely on each others footsteps. The beginning of 1886 was a time of great depression in the shipping trade. Liverpool and Bootle suffered heavily. A relief committee was formed, and subscriptions solicited under the auspices of the town authorities. Ministers and other benevolent gentlemen were asked to

investigate the cases before granting relief tickets.
Mr. Briscombe quickly joined this benevolent
association, and rendered substantial help in a
variety of ways. His ministerial white tie did not
hold him back from the crowded streets and alleys
where want, and crime, and ignorance huddled
together in the foul darkness. The writer regrets his
inability to describe the scenes witnessed by Mr.
Briscombe during his seven continuous hours of
visiting in Dundas-street, in which there was something that reminded one of Dante's 'Hell.' The
buildings in this street with the cellar dwellings are
four stories ; the families do not live in houses but
in rooms.

Squalid Homes.

In these rooms Mr. Briscombe found many who
were slowly starving; who had no food, fire, nor
furniture, but sat there in a silent torpor, which was
very striking. In the eyes and brows of some of
them hung the gloomiest expression, not of anger,
but of grief, shame, distress, and weariness, that
returned a glance which seemed to say, " Do not look
at us." One room was the home of a wretched family;
the man was a willing worker, but could not get
anything to do. The room, apparent'y, was bare of
everything, except a box and a stool. Think of the
man sitting on his box watching his children sleep on
a plank-bed, covered perhaps with his coat. As the
night wears on, the biting east winds blow down the

chimney ; the frost of a bitter March morning creeps in through the crevices of the door and window. Still the man sits there on his box, sleeping a short, broken sleep, numbed with the cold, stiffened and aching. Then at last, the cold grey rays of daylight peep in through the window-panes. Through the dim light, the forms of the sleeping children are seen nestling for warmth close together. He awakes the children, who shiver with cold as they gather around the dead fire, and then go into the street without breakfast. The man goes out upon his fruitless search for employment. Hours are spent in trudging from dock to dock ; the evening comes again, and he goes home overwhelmed with disappointment after disappointment. No wonder that the women and children, under such circumstances, should gather around Mr. Briscombe and say, "Come to our room." No wonder that Mr. Briscombe should continue his visits and relief in this street from ten o'clock in the morning until five o'clock in the afternoon, neither partaking of food nor rest, until he was almost fainting from exhaustion. At last when he informed them that he was really unable to continue longer in his visits, the people thronged around him, and followed him up the street, at the top of which was a bread shop. He entered, and gave each of them numbering about twenty, a loaf of bread. It was this memorable day's work that moved him to begin giving a free breakfast at his own residence in Stanley-road.

How Mr. Briscombe Fed Upwards of 6,000 People.

The following account will show how this philanthropic work was appreciated by the starving poor. The free breakfast consisted of a mug of tea, and two thick slices of bread and butter, which was given to every poor person who applied at his house for relief. The procession of wretched applicants continually increased. Sometimes as many as 200 partook of the meal in one morning, among which were some strange and woeful specimens of humanity, such as would have challenged Hogarth's pencil to caricature. Mr. Briscombe having a large garden at the back of his house, was accustomed to admit not more than 40 at a time, limited to the crockery at his command. This took up all the mornings of Mrs. Briscombe, himself, and servant, whilst it lasted. His friends at length resolved to lessen his work and share the toil, and forthwith united in opening a soup kitchen at the Wesleyan schoolroom, which continued until milder weather and improving trade rendered it no longer necessary. On pressing Mr. Briscombe to state the aggregate number of breakfasts given during this period, he permitted me to read the record from his diary, kept at the time, and on summing up the numbers amounted to upwards of 6,000.

His ministry at Bootle was in other respects even in its flow, but continuously acceptable. He discharged all the general duties of his office so as to win high esteem for his character and great regard for his services in the pastorate and the pulpit.

THE BURNLEY CIRCUIT.

In September, 1887, Mr. Briscombe, having some time previously accepted an invitation to become its second minister, removed to Burnley. During the former half of his term of service there he threw very great energy into his work, and added largely to the duties of his own circuit by undertaking extra work of a special kind in other circuits. Feeling his strength fully restored, he unwisely multiplied his public engagements, and infused into them so much vocal vigour that at length the former symptoms of exhaustion, after public work, began to appear. The first sign of the returning debility was felt after preaching Sunday school anniversary sermons in another circuit. A little rest, or comparatively small restraint on his public duties would probably have averted anything worse. But he had involved himself in such a multiplicity of engagements, and had such an ardent desire to fulfil the obligations undertaken, that in the attempt to do so he succumbed. The climax of the calamity was reached the Sunday following the one just mentioned. On that day he was called out at 8 a.m. to visit a dying woman. He preached at Fulledge Chapel in the morning at 10-30, gave an address at Whittlefield School early in the afternoon, preached at a mission-room at Fulledge at half-past three, visited and prayed with two families immediately after, then took a hasty tea and preached again at Fulledge Chapel in the evening. The address and all the three sermons were delivered with as much vigour as he had ever displayed in public work, and it was not till the close of the evening service that a rapid reaction set in. Even then he had to administer the Lord's Supper, and the exhaustion was such that he could not speak in giving the elements, was obliged to conclude abruptly, and could not pronounce the benediction. He was assisted into the vestry, where he was obliged to recline for a long time until, with the aid of restoratives, he so far rallied as to be able to be taken home in a cab. Duty had to be suspended for a while, and when he resumed work he was not able for a long period to conduct a service quite through. His colleagues in the ministry displayed great kindness in relieving him as much as possible from duty, and the Rev. J. W. Blackett generously rendered special help in this respect. The circuit, too, remembering the ardour with which he had attempted to do his work when in health, showed great sympathy and consideration for him in his weakness to the very end of his term. He was able, during the last year of his being in the circuit, to fulfil in general his Sunday appointments, with the aid of someone to conduct the prayer or read the lessons, and to fulfil under certain limitations the duties of his pastorate. Thus in the contrasted experiences of strength and weakness his ministry in this circuit was brought to a close with the mingled feelings of high regard for his varied talents and fervent zeal, along with sympathy for his weakness and respect for the moral influence of his character.

PRESTON WESLEY CIRCUIT.

Mr. Briscombe accepted the pressing call of the Wesley Circuit to become its superintendent minister, in 1890. He commenced his labours in Wesley Chapel by preaching the Sunday School Anniversary Sermons on the first Sunday in September, to crowded congregations. His sermons were marked by great energy of thought, combined with beautiful and tasteful illustrations, which impressed the people that he was just such a preacher as this circuit required. At the same time, it was feared that his health was not of that robust character which the work in Preston would require; the penalty of labour beyond his strength in his previous circuit having caused the physical weakness. The friends showed great willingness to render him all the aid that he desired to avert another break-down; but now that he has entered on the second year of his ministry in the circuit, it is satisfactory to know that his health and vigour appear to be fully restored. He enters on his circuit duties as an heir enters on his estate. The Church is his study, his library, his creed, his meat and drink; and he truly lives in and for his work. He is below the average height in stature and physical proportion. Diminutive men are smarter, as a rule, than those of the bulky and adipose kind. John Wesley was a small man, but remarkable for his intellectual vigour and religious activity. It is said that he never weighed more than eight stones. Dr. Dallinger, the scientific divine, and Sir Garnet Wolseley, the greatest modern military hero, and Dr. Lees, the distinguished Temperance controversialist, are all men under the average height and weight; but it is impossible to measure their magnitude of influence. There is nothing pretentious in Mr. Briscombe's appearance; nothing specially ecclesiastical in his dress or bearing, so that in the street he looks almost as much like one of the general public as a minister. His natural capacities have been well stored by study. He is neither fussy in manner nor conceited in his opinions, nor addicted to the display of authority; nor yet fond of brandishing the sword of defiance. He has got charity in his speech as well as in his purse. He has little of the self-will that frustrates matured counsels; is free from the stubbornness that refuses in disputed matters to yield the slightest concession. All who know Mr. Briscombe give him credit for a desire to do his duty. He neither courts popularity nor resents criticism; he throws his whole soul into his office, and his heart expands with the enlarging schemes of the circuit.

Social Meetings.

During the first year that Mr. Briscombe was in the Wesley Circuit, an unusually large number of social meetings were held, preceded by tea or followed by supper, at which he frequently presided.

The attendance often amounted to about three hundred people, and the special financial object of the meetings was to aid a large circuit scheme to remove debts from two town chapels, as well as to raise a fund for the building of a New Chapel at Ashton, as a Centenary memorial of John Wesley's death.

Mr. Briscombe's cheerful countenance, and sometimes playful genius, with the happy effusions of his ready tongue, shed animation on these gatherings, and greatly enlivened the proceedings. His speeches are remarkable for good nature, aptness, and vivacity, which give an excellent spirit and tone to the meeting. He contrives to make every one at ease, and to call forth the best energies of all. A Highland elder, describing the ministerial succession in his parish, said: "The one we had last was a minister, but not a man; the one before him was a man, but not a minister; while the one we have now is neither a man nor a minister." Mr. Briscombe is both a man and a minister; he mixes freely with every class of his people, and is ready and willing to discuss their questions. He speedily gains the esteem and affection of all who have an opportunity of intercourse with him. His general disposition is eminently kind, candid, and conciliatory. His ready wit, accompanied by keen discernment of character, would make him formidable in the use of sarcasm or ridicule, but we do not remember him to have used this gift in any way calculated to give pain. Mr. Briscombe fulfils his position as the leader of his people, co-operating with their labours, whilst rendering valuable aid in maturing and guiding their schemes.

VISITING THE SICK.

The writer has not had opportunity to judge of his skill and fidelity in speaking pointedly to the conscience in private; but he has heard the testimony of those who did sustain that important relation, and their testimony was that his visits in the sick chamber were peculiarly acceptable, not only on account of their sympathising kindness, but because of the tact and judgment with which his conversation and his prayers were adapted to the circumstances of the case.

His social intercourse is peculiarly attractive. There is a beaming welcome in his countenance. In his conversation there is a smartness that ever keeps you on the alert. In the presence of the young he displays the cheerfulness of one belonging to their own age and station. He is always happy when surrounded by young people. On the platform and in the pulpit he addresses them with an affection that arrests their attention and touches their sensibilities.

MR. BRISCOMBE AS A PREACHER.

The earlier part of the service is conducted with impressiveness; his prayers are neither long nor common-place, but reverent, pointed, and sympathetic His lessons are usually read by one of the office

bearers of the church. He availed himself of this
help in the first instance when he was in a weak
state of health, but still continues it as a means of
utilising the latent ability of his lay brethren, as
well as of conserving his full strength for the
sermon. His enunciation is distinct without undue
elevation of voice, but we understand he was
formerly more vehement, especially in winding up a
discourse. It is evident that the strength and force
of Mr. Briscombe's preaching lie chiefly in the
substance and texture of his sermon rather than in
any special grace in delivery, though this is by no
means wanting. His object is to emphasise and
throw light on those elements of truth which have
most appositeness to the thought and life of the age.
He eyes what is going on outside, and selects and
preaches what bears on the current needs of life.
There is no overloading, nor yet any deficiency of
matter. He sets forth the chief point of his subject
with clearness, and presses it upon one's acceptance
in a manner that will scarcely allow refusal. He
possesses a remarkable facility in tracing the
relative dependence of truths upon each other, and
has a clear and vigorous judgment, which enables
him readily to apprehend matters difficult of investigation. His arguments are well stated, clearly
arranged, and expressed in homely, but not un-
dignified language, Mr. Briscombe never seems to
forget that his business as a preacher of the Gospel is
to " persuade men." In this department his

resources are very varied. It has been said that some painters are only successful with a gloomy sky and a restless sea, others with green fields and running brooks, so some preachers can only produce terror, and others only tears, but Mr. Briscombe has both sublimity and tenderness. He is never dull, but always to the point, speaking like a man whose heart was stirred by a lofty topic. He seizes the attention of one class of hearers after another, and keeps all on the alert for what may come next. The subject of our sketch lives among the big writers ancient and modern, and introduces them to his audience. These references do not interrupt the current of his own thoughts; but are impressively incorporated with them. Hence the variety and interest of his discourse. The thoroughness of his investigation of subjects shows that with him it is a matter of conscience not to offer to God that which costs him nothing. His subjects are well studied, and it is evident that they are extemporaneously delivered.

The following is an extract from one of his sermons on " The evidences of a Deity." It is taken from the *Preston Guardian*, November 21st, 1891. Those will understand the sermon best who can recall the very tone and emphasis of the speaker, who were listeners rather than readers. It would have been easy to have selected a more brilliant passage from other sermons, but we have this to hand ; we might have given others, but our limits do

not permit. There is also something very character-
istic of the preacher in what we cite :—

"On Sunday evening, at Wesley Chapel, North-
road, the Rev. W. Briscombe delivered a sermon on
' The existence of a Deity—its evidences and lessons.'
Basing his remarks on Romans i., 19-20, he said the
belief in a Deity was the foundation doctrine of every
religion. It was a doctrine of the most vital importance, seeing that the duties they owed to God
were based upon that primal belief. The text called
attention to two great lines of proof respecting the
existence of a Deity, the evidence being supplied in
the first place by the constitution of the natural
world, and in the second by man's moral nature.
The passage stated that the visible things of God
" were clearly seen from the creation of the world,
being understood by the things that are made." The
evidence of intelligence in the construction and order
of the universe involved that behind all those orderly
phenomena there was a personal intelligence. St.
Paul said that every house was builded by some man,
but he that built all things was God. From that
striking analogy, the preacher showed that the discovery of a perfect house in a lonely desert would, by
the evidences of design, adaptation, and utility to an
end, in its doors, windows, staircases, roof, and other
appurtenances, lead one to the conclusion that it had
been built by some living human being. By a parity
of reasoning, the manifestation of infinitely higher
forms of intelligence in the material universe, led to

the conclusion that a living and divine intelligence had originated it. It was not necessary to have an ocular demonstration of living intelligence in order to believe in it, for to see living intelligence was a simple impossibility. The anatomist might dissect the brain, but could never discover the living intelligence. Only in its manifestations upon matter could a living intelligence be discerned. If one desired to see Shakespeare they could only refer him to his writings; or to see Sir Christopher Wren, they could but point him to St. Paul's Cathedral and kindred works. Geologists had inferred the existence of intelligent men in the indefinite ages of the past, from the finding of the flint knives which bore the faintest possible traces of art. If such a feeble sign of intelligence was regarded as an argument for the remote existence of man, how much more were the infinite marks of wisdom and adaptation in the universe solid evidences of the existence of an intelligent Creator. The origin of life was inexplicable apart from the belief in an intelligent Creator. It was admitted by all scientists that there was a period when no life existed on our globe. The question was, how did the abundant life now existent originate? Only three theories could be possible—either life was self-originated, or some meteorite had been projected to this globe bearing in it the germs of life, or else there was an intelligent Creator. The theory of the self-origination of life assumed that life could act before it was brought into existence, which was impossible, and was pronounced scientifically untrue. At one time, nevertheless, Professor Tyndall did teach that life was self-originated, but scientific evidence had since then constrained him to acknowledge and recall his error, and all scientists now agreed that life sprang only from antecedent life. The theory of life projected by a meteorite was equally untenable, because the speed at which it would be projected would generate such an amount of heat as to extinguish any germs of life that might be on it. The only rational theory left to account for life was the volition of an intelligent Creator. Evolution, as taught by Darwin, did not attempt to account for the origin of life, but assumed a few primal forms of life to begin with. The next argument of the preacher was the proof of the existence of a Deity from man's moral nature. The text said, ' That which may be known of God is manifest in them,' that was, in man. Man was the image of his Maker, reflecting His moral nature. He was the only God-conscious being in this world. A great German philosopher remarked, ' There are two things which impress me above all others—the starry worlds above me and the moral nature within me.' An ancient Greek sage said, ' If you would find God, look within.' It was to be expected that as man was God's chief work in this world the divine impress would be most deeply stamped upon him. The universal belief in a Deity—either good or bad, great or small—was a natural evidence of God's existence. It was impossible that a universal instinct should be untrue. A few exceptions to the rule have been stated, but they could all be adequately met; and in no wise did they invalidate the general rule that man instinctively believed in a power higher than himself. Kant regarded the possession of a moral nature by man as the strongest proof of the existence of a Deity. The preacher then called attention to the practical lessons of the subject."

MR. BRISCOMBE A CHAMPION OF THEOLOGY.

Contest after contest on Biblical questions found Mr. Briscombe in the front rank in the arena of controversy, battering down error and false doctrines, undaunted, fluent, eloquent, convinced, and convincing, rolling back the waves of prejudice. Advancing onward until every obstruction was swept away, and the mists of ignorance were dissipated by the blaze of light and truth.

In addition to Mr. Briscombe's popularity as a lecturer on theological subjects, he has, on many occasions, delivered lectures on social topics, displaying large sympathy with the varied conditions of human life, aptly illustrated by telling incidents.

He is a total abstainer of long standing, and holds the temperance creed that intoxicating liquors, as beverages, are neither necessary, beneficial, nor safe.

MR. BRISCOMBE'S POLITICAL VIEWS.

He thinks great reforms are needed in our methods

of caring for the poor. He would have waste lands reclaimed both in the interior of the country and from estuaries of many of our rivers. He would have all the able-bodied unemployed engaged in this work at a reasonable pay, and would have the Government to claim all foreshore rights as the rights of the community. He has a high regard for the Queen, and prefers limited Monarchy to Republicanism for Great Britain. Whilst preferring his own Church to any other, he thinks highly of the Church of England, and has no desire to see it either disestablished or disendowed. A few minor reforms he deems desirable, and would especially like to see an acceptable settlement of the tithes question. He thinks that those who assail the Church of England on account of her large emoluments and overlook the great injury inflicted by the entailed system of the country, "strain at a gnat and swallow a camel." He adheres to the historic theology of Christianity, as expressed in the historical creeds of the Church of England, regarding these as vital doctrines of Christian belief. Lesser questions he leaves open to difference of opinion. He does not agree with those who find fault with the Queen's Civil List allowances, nor with those who condemn the salaries of the Episcopate as unjust. Nor, is he in favour of destroying the system of landlordism, and merging all land into possession of the State. He thinks every man becomes a better citizen who becomes a landlord. He also entertains a high regard for our municipal institutions and for the House of Commons, as containing the representatives of the people, with power of legislation. He thinks that merchants, manufacturers, importers, exporters, and all who by enterprise find employment for others, rank amongst public benefactors, and are worthy of success for aiding others to find employment. The only classes of the community for whom he has no sentiment of regard, and who, as a class, render the least service to society and reap from it the largest advantages, are the entailed classes. He holds that the greatest social evil in society, and that which is the most fertile cause of nearly all other evils, in a direct or indirect form, is a system which entails more than half of the land of the country to less than a thousand people. He regards this as a violation of the law of natural, revealed, and social justice. He thinks the antiquity of the institution does not condone its iniquity. Whatever merits the feudal system had in its origin they are now lost, and all its evils are aggravated. In its best days it regarded duty as being linked to privilege, and the feudal lord kept the poor on his estate, provided a proportion of the army at his own expense, acted as its general in war, and exercised judicial functions in peace. All these duties are now foregone, and the public pays for the poor, for the army, for its generals, and for judges who administer our laws. But all its privileges are increased by the industry of the community, and the

men who have done least, as a class, to advance the
welfare of the country are reaping at an increasing
rate the unearned increment, whilst the commercial
and industrial classes are entering on a keener
struggle for existence. Many who complain of the
salaries of the bishops forget that all of them
together do not receive one-tenth part of some members of the entailed classes ; and they forget that
many of the entailed classes receive a larger income
than our gracious Queen. The Queen and the
bishops render great and important service to
society, but the entailed classes, in virtue of their
position, render none. He regards the Scriptures as
giving high sanction to royalty, but he holds that
such a system as that which the entailed classes
enjoy is against Scripture—against natural justice,
and hurtful to the best interests of society. He
thinks the Irish question and many other questions
of great national urgency would soon receive a
happy solution if the laws of entail and primogeniture were repealed, and a simple Act of Parliament
passed to make every acre of land in the country abso-
lutely freehold. He is also of opinion that the removing of the unjust and obnoxious laws of entail and
primogeniture, which were made by the entailed
classes alone, and for their own benefit, at a time
when representative Parliaments were unknown,
would have a most beneficial influence over the
country, both socially and religiously. Whilst not
advocating the disendowment of the entailed classes,

he does not think that would be unjust. The Church of Ireland has been disendowed, and the English Bishops have been in part disendowed, and the Parliament of the entailed classes sanctioned both these schemes. It could not, therefore, be regarded as unjust for the Parliament to treat the " lay lords " as they have helped to treat the spiritual lords.

He thinks favourably of an Upper House of Parliament, but would have it composed of life peers, who have earned their position by display of ability, or by special service to the country. Believing, as he does, that the entailed system is a gross injustice to the community, he has no esteem for the hereditary titles of honour of those who live by what he considers the greatest system of social injustice in existence.[A]

Mr. Briscombe would have been a worthy comrade of John Hampden, John Selden, and John Pym. He possesses the very spirit of the puritan leaders. He has their brave and honest heart, their sound and steady judgment, their manly hatred of oppression, of bad laws, and bad government. He wields the sword of just thinking, of manly fighting, of pure living, and of stern resisting of all evil. But peace is his atmosphere, his yearning desire is to do his duty—and who can go higher?

MR. BRISCOMBE'S BOOK.

In fulfilling our promise to give some extracts from the Rev. W. Briscombe's Book, "Hades,

---

A. From " Local Men " in *Bootle Times*, August 6th, 1886.

Heaven, and Gehenna, (or Hell)," we must first point out to the readers that the space before us will only permit brief quotations. Doctrinally he is with the new school. The new school is manifestly the old school over again, the truths of the Gospel must emphatically maintain their objective reality. That is to say, think of them as we will, they are independent and unchanging principles. There they are, like the fire cloud of Israel in the wilderness, shining upon our pathway by their own light, themselves unaltered by the imperfections of our vision, by the coloured glasses we may choose to look through, or by the refracting mists that float around us. From this cause eternal truths do not look just the same to all christians. Seen, they are, more or less, by all christians; rejoiced in and loved by all christians; but under rather different aspects, from different standpoints, and in different lights.

In this book he gives his complete views of the subject of a future life, and contends that the human spirit is inherently immortal, in opposition to the theory of annihilationists. He sets forth the doctrine that Hades is an intermediate state distinct from heaven or hell, and that it was the abode of all departed spirits, whether good or bad, until the death of the Redeemer. He regards the death of Christ as marking a new era in the condition of departed saints, raising them from the lower condition of Hades to the higher condition of a blissful abode in heaven. He also holds that the greatest benefit of Christ's death to living saints is the privilege of going direct to heaven at death. Whilst "the spirits of just men are made perfect" in heavenly bliss, he maintains that bodily bliss of the highest order will be added to the saints after their resurrection. The unsaved he regards as abiding in the intermediate state of Hades until the resurrection and judgment, when they will be cast into the Gehenna of actual and final punishment.

The following is an extract from his discourse on " Heaven: the Nature, Degrees and Duration of its Bliss":—

"(a) *As a Place, the Heavenly world is BETTER.*

"In speaking of the abode of the saints after their departure hence, the Sacred Book defines it as '*A better* country, that is, a Heavenly.'—Heb. xi., 16. To illustrate this principle let us think of the richest and purest joys derivable from this world, and eliminating therefrom every drawback, let us imagine these joys to be immensely intensified and perpetually prolonged, and we form a just conception of that kind of joy which shall be derivable from Heaven as the region of our abode. Our present world yields, through laborious toil, enjoyable sustenance; it has scenes of exquisite beauty which, at limited times, we may occasionally see; it has, at certain seasons of the year, a sky of transparent clearness, or occasionally adorned with the variegated colours of the summer clouds; it has, on rare occasions, a balmy atmosphere, which alike gives pleasure to the body and to the act of respiration ; it has trees, herbs, and flowers, which for a limited period of the year exhale their fragant odours, whilst they adorn the landscape for the eye ; and it has rills, and zephyrs, and songs of birds, to relieve its dulness, and to charm the ear with joyous sounds !

"But these earthly joys are rare in their occurrence and short in their duration. Even when these objects surround us, through affliction, or present troubles, or future fears, we may be unable to enjoy them. Our earthly joy is, indeed, commonly far short of what we have sketched as possible. But the highest joys of this earthly world are far exceeded by the kindred joys of the celestial world.

" In Eden, which God fitted up for man's reception, we have an indication that God designed a pleasant place of abode for sinless man. When man sinned, the ground was cursed for man's sake. The world in which he lived became blighted by his transgression. It is God's design to recover man from sin, and thereby lift him to a world where the blight of sin does not extend. Here, men live together in cities, or dwell more detached, in rural parts, as may suit their convenience or pleasure. Each of these conditions of life has its own special advantage, and each may be changed for the pleasures of variety. Heaven has something corresponding to each of these aspects of earthly life. The same thing will, in principle, obtain, if not in precise mode. Hence we find it called both the 'better country' and 'the city of the living God.' As a country, all its scenery is charming, its sky is ever clear, its air is always balmy, its odours are continually exhaling, and its sounds are perpetually delighting. As a city, its proportions are beautiful, its buildings are majestic, its river is pure, its walls are of precious stones, its gates of pearl, and its pavement of gold. If such descriptions be figurative, they embody the real truth. The best, most precious, and most beautiful things of earth are employed to denote the better things in the Heavenly world. Hence to the persecuted Hebrews, who lost their best earthly comforts in serving their Master, the apostle wrote the animating words, 'Ye have in Heaven a *better* and an enduring substance. —Heb. x., 34.

" The eye of man may have gazed on the most charming scenes of nature ; the ear of man may have listened to the finest descriptions that words, or similitudes could express ; and the imagination of man may have been trained to its most exalted powers of conception ; yet, in each, the reality of Heavenly bliss will be *better* than has been seen, heard, or imagined ; for 'Eye hath not seen, nor ear heard, neither have entered into the heart of man, the things which God hath prepared for them that love Him.'—1 Cor. ii., 9."

The following passages are taken from his discourse on " Hell; The Placeof Final Retribution, :

The Nature, Proportion, and Duration of its Punishment " : —

" I.—*We shall investigate the Nature of its Punishments.*

" There is no doubt that many Christian ministers and authors have delivered their sentiments on this subject in a very indiscreet and unguarded manner. The hasty application of Scripture metaphors in a literal sense, and their sincere but injudicious elaboration of them as a motive to turn from sin, have led them to many extremes of expression alike revolting to reason and contrary to a sober interpretation of the Word of God. The popular idea of Hell, largely arising from this cause, is that there is a literal pit of fire and brimstone, whose fierce flames and stifling fumes inflict perpetual agony upon the transgressors. The author at once proceeds to avow that, in his opinion, *the Scriptures do nowhere teach that the punishments of Hell consist, either in whole or in part, of literal fire !*

" That the lost sinners to be sentenced to Gehenna, or Hell, will endure severe *internal* punishment is declared by Christ when He says of them : ' Their *worm* dieth not.' His apparent reference was to the gnawing of their consciences by remorse as a worm devours a corpse. It is not ' *the* worm,' but ' *their* worm,' indicating that it springs from the sinner himself and is the just reaction of wrong-doing upon his own mind !

" In this respect it unfolds the great principle of

the Divine administration in regard to future punishments. As virtue is said to be its own reward, so vice is, with equal truth, its own punishment. It is written : ' Whatsoever a man soweth *that* shall he also reap.'—Gal. vi., 7. The meaning is that in a future life man will reap something corresponding in kind to the actions performed in the present life. The connection between the seed and the crop sets forth the connection between what we sow in time and what we reap in eternity. The crop is the *outgrowth* of the seed. If a man sows wheat he reaps wheat, but if he sow darnel, cockle, poppies, thorns, or thistles, he reaps the same kind of thing in harvest. In the harvest of eternity the same principle obtains. ' *Whatsoever* a man soweth *that* shall he also reap.'

"The *Appetites* shall be punished in the reaction of their abuse. As our Lord represents the rich man in Hades suffering in his tongue, who had most indulged in his appetite, so this sets forth a deeper reaction that will obtain in the final Gehenna, when the resurrection body will feel a keener sense of pain than could the disembodied spirit in Hades. The drunkard will no doubt experience in his resurrection body the burning thirst of intemperance, without the means of its gratification or appeasement. The glutton will feel something analogous to the keen longing for a diet which he is not privileged to enjoy. The abused appetites which gave him pleasure, in a sinful life on earth, turn round to become his tormentors in Gehenna! He cannot complain that God is unjust, because he generated and nursed the vipers which now turn round and sting him. He became the slave of such sinful pleasures, and now they have assumed the tyranny over him. *Before*, they ministered to his sinful pleasure; *now*, they minister to his judicial pain!

" The *Passions* too of the transgressor shall, by their perversion, become the agents of his punishment. The abuse of the natural passions, by the indulgence of those ' fleshy lusts which war against the soul,' shall bring a just entail of woe in the future life. We read of those who gave themselves up to a life of impurity that ' God gave them up to vile affections.'—Rom. i., 26. His reason for doing so is declared to be their persistence in those base desires. ' God gave them up to uncleanliness through their lust.'—Rom. i., 24. What God did to them, on earth, sets forth the divine principle of punishment in Gehenna. In their resurrection bodies their lusts will inhere, and the depraved sympathy of the mind will goad them to desires which cannot be attained, and leave them the pain of sin without any of its pleasure. Their experience in this respect may be expressed in the language of Ezekiel xx.. 43: ' Ye shall loathe yourselves in your own sight for all your evils which ye have committed.'

" The *Tempers* also of the evil-doer will react to his punishment. Their anarchy will destroy his peace, and their chronic irritation fret his mind. 'Envy, hatred, malice, and all uncharitableness' will reign supreme. It is a pure fiction on the part of the poet to say 'Devil with devil damned firm concord holds.' It is contrary to nature that a corrupt tree should bring forth good fruit. Any concord that obtains amongst demons must arise from policy and not from inherent disposition. It must be a temporary truce to avert a mighty evil. If there be a momentary concord, from the motive of mutual benefit, it can never be, in perverted natures, from the sense of right. Or, if, for a season, it be obtained from fear, it can never, even for a season, spring from love! If saints are to be like the angels, then, on this principle sinners will be like the demons. Let us suppose that all the worst-tempered men in the world were constrained to dwell together. Evil tempers in acting on evil tempers would receive the greater irritation, and brutalities contending with brutalities would be awfully intensified! He who is the prey of such evil tempers may well exclaim with Milton's Satan : 'Myself am Hell!'

"The *Memory* of the transgressor shall further add to the severity of his woe in the Gehenua to come. Memory is the power of retaining the past and may either come at our call, or force itself on our attention despite our will. Its tale is always true. It can only recollect what has occurred, it is able only to recall what has transpired. A man's memory will reflect his conduct and reproduce beyond his death the events of a former life. To the rich man in Hades Abraham said : 'Son, remember thy lifetime!' The sinner doomed to Gehenna can only remember life as he lived it. He can only reflect on what actually took place. The evil which brings him to Gehenna is the evil which will be most vividly remembered there. To reflect on our folly quenches our joy. To dwell on our misconduct saddens our mind. But on earth there are many opiates to a conscience charged with guilt. Pleasure, business, or travel may divert a guilty soul from remembering its sin, but the like possibilities will not operate in perdition. Memory will then be burdened with a load of painful recollections from which it cannot obtain release.

"The *Conscience* is closely allied with the memory, and will minister increasing anguish to the mind of the lost. It is said 'the best things when perverted become the worst.' Conscience, which is the best friend of the saint, becomes the worst foe of the sinner. Origen, in the third century says : 'When the soul has gathered together a multitude of evil works, and an abundance of sins against itself, at a suitable time, all that assembly of evils boils up to punishment.' He also adds that, 'The conscience will see a kind of history, as it were, of all the foul, and shameful, and unholy deeds which it has done exposed before its eyes ; then the conscience, itself harassed, and pierced by its own goads, becomes an accuser and witness against itself.'—De Prin., Bk, II., x., 4. Conscience on earth may be silenced, but in Gehenna it can neither be seared, gagged, nor stupified. It will speak out in retaliation for its enforced silence and stir up the feelings of self-loathing, self-reproach, and remorse. In this case the accuser is within, and the man is ever at war with himself!

"To sum up then the rational and Scriptural view of the nature of future punishments after the Judgment Day, this epitome may suffice : The wicked are at present detained in Hades, without any judicial punishment. After the Judgment Day they will be consigned to Gehenna, to which event the Saviour refers when he says : 'Depart, ye cursed, into everlasting fire prepared for the devil and his angels.' The place called Gehenna, to which they will be confined, will be a dreary, desolate, and cheerless abode. Eternal night settles on their region, for to them 'is reserved the blackness of darkness for ever.' 'The fire' that is threatened is a metaphor of divine displeasure emanating from God, and falling upon their guilty souls. 'Their worm' is the inward grief they feel, arising from the internal reaction of their own sins. All the sorrows that afflict their minds, all the evil appetites tempers, and passions which they feel, are the outgrowth of their probationary life on earth. Memory and conscience are the self-accusers of the sinner, and the just vindicators of the Deity. These admit the fact of their guilt and the justice of their doom. These will confess, as did the penitent thief, for himself and fellow sufferer,—' We indeed (suffer) justly; for we receive the due reward of our deeds.'—Lu. xxiii., 42."A

A " Hades, Heaven, and Gehenna (or Hell)," with a controversial Lecture on " Man's Immortality," by the Rev. Walter Brisconin, 2s. 6d. ; or by Parcel post, 2s. 9d. Sold by W. Pilkington, 101, Friargate, Preston.

CONTENTS.

THE MAKERS OF METHODISM IN PRESTON, AND THE RELATION OF METHODISM TO THE TEMPERANCE MOVEMENT: By W. Pilkington. With Illustrations, 3s. 6d.

WHAT THE PRESS SAYS.

The *Methodist Recorder*, May 21st, 1891, says :—
" We are always ready to give a hearty welcome to new volumes of local Methodist history. So many of the heroes of the early time have passed, or are rapidly passing away, and with them, in many cases, vast funds of unrecorded fact with regard to the rise and early incidents of Methodism in their own parts of the country, that it is matter for great thankfulness when either ministers or laymen manifest sufficient public spirit to perform the usually unremunerative task of gathering, collating and authenticating such details as can be obtained, and giving them a permanent form. Mr. Pilkington, a Preston local preacher in the prime of life, was led to undertake this task, we understand, by the request to read a paper on the history of Methodism in Preston up to the Centenary year, 1838, at the Jubilee of Wesley Chapel in 1888. He was subsequently desired to print the paper in an enlarged form, bringing the story up to the present day. Mr. Pilkington has laid not merely his native town, but the whole connexion under considerable obligation by his labours. The careful historian describes *seriatim* the rise and progress of our Church in each of the places included in the plans of the two circuits, and further enriches his volume with interesting biographical sketches, and in several instances portraits of local Methodist worthies. He gives also *facsimiles* of old circuit plans, a complete list of ministers who have laboured in the town, and of Presidents of the Conference from the beginning,

with a good index. The last 100 pages of the book are devoted to a sketch of the relation of Methodism to the Temperance Movement. The Church has received much obloquy from Temperance speakers of late years for the step-motherly attitude she is said to have assumed towards the Temperance cause in its infancy, and doubtless there may be found much reason for the charge. But Temperance in Preston, at least, seems to have been to a very considerable extent an offshoot of Methodism. The first Preston Temperance reformer was Henry Anderton, a Methodist local preacher, and in 1830, or 1831, he, with James Teare, another Methodist local preacher from the Isle of Man, were among the founders of the first Preston Temperance Society. William Pollard, yet another local preacher, followed hard after them, and Richard Turner, a Wesleyan Sunday-school teacher, was the inventor of the word Teetotal. The first public meeting of the Preston Temperance Society was held—let the fact be remembered—in the Lord-street Wesleyan Schoolroom on Good Friday, 1832, and was presided over by the Rev. Charles Radcliffe. In many respects this Temperance section of the volume is of even greater interest than the former part, and once more, in closing the book, we thank Mr. Pilkington for the service he has rendered to Methodism by its production."

The *Methodist Times*, Sep. 17th, 1891, says:—"To this bulky and well-printed volume there is a somewhat lengthy sub-title : 'The relation of Methodism to the Temperance and Teetotal Movements, Adventure, Enterprise, and Noble Deeds of Preston Methodist Celebrities.' We are somewhat late in noticing Mr. Pilkington's book, but none the less we give it a very hearty welcome. It would have been an immense pity to allow this store of good things to pass into forgetfulness for want of a faithful scribe. Of course there is a great deal in the book that is purely technical, if we may apply that term to long lists of names. But even the technical part has its value, and will provide very useful hints whenever exhaustive enquiry becomes necessary. As for the rest of the volume, we could wish that Mr. Clapham would present the book to every member of the home missionary deputations, with the express stipulation that they should make a very religious use of its treasures in every speech they may deliver. When there arises the Dean Ramsey of Methodism he will bless Mr. Pilkington. We may add, further, that the book is enriched by many full-page illustrations, and by a short preface from the Rev. Charles Garrett."

Onward, the organ of the Preston and District Band of Hope Union, March, 1891, says :—"We cannot conceive of a book which could in a greater degree interest the teetotallers and especially the Methodist teetotallers of Preston than this. It is well got up and well illustrated, and from a perusal of an advance copy we can vouch that the author, Mr. Wm. Pilkington, has spared no pains and shirked no amount of research to make the book graphic, complete in detail, and profitable to the reader. To deal with the whole book would be a task far beyond the limits of the space at our disposal. The part most intensely interesting to us is of course the one dealing with Methodism's relations to the two movements—temperance and teetotalism. He has devoted himself to proving that instead of being covered with reproach for its opposition in the early stages of the temperance and teetotal movements, the Methodist Church has not only been favourable to these reforms, but that her sons have been their originators and founders. We must admit that Mr. Pilkington presents a strong case, and that he backs up his statements by references which are entirely unexceptional. 'Honour where honour is due' is no doubt an excellent maxim, and Mr. Pilkington is quite within his right in endeavouring to remove the stigma of reproach which has been so long affixed to his Church for her former attitude to our movement. Having proved the modern temperance and the total abstinence movements to have originated in Methodist circles in Preston, Mr. Pilkington proceeds to give us an account of the drinking habits and customs of the people in 1830. The picture drawn is a fearful one, and we feel relieved when he brings on the scene, his Seven Methodist Temperance Pioneers. The hero of the temperance movement is Henry Anderton, and the champion of total abstinence James Teare, both Methodist local preachers. These, with William Pollard, Moses Holden, Thomas Whittaker (all local preachers), Dicky Turner (a Methodist Sunday-school teacher), and the Rev. C. Ratcliffe make up Mr. Pilkington's Seven Men of Preston. The description of the work done by these men and fellow-workers is a most inspiriting one, and the book should be read by everyone interested in temperance work if only for the sake of obtaining a fresh impetus to their zeal and determination by reading of the wonderful doings and sayings of these early pioneers."

The *Preston Chronicle*, May 2nd, 1891, says:—"Mr. Pilkington's book is what it claims to be—a record of facts that should be deeply interesting not only to Methodists, but to members of every Christian community. Beyond its value as an historical record of the progress of Methodism in this part of the country, Mr. Pilkington's book has many other features which will commend it. In addition to some useful statistics relative to the position of local Methodism, it comprises a complete roll of the preachers who have laboured in Preston and the neighbourhood from 1753 downwards, and a list of Conference presidents since 1791. The work is neatly got up, well printed, and most admirably illustrated. On the whole, we consider that the Wesleyans of Preston and district are to be congratulated in having secured in Mr. Pilkington an able, intelligent historian, who has rescued their ancient records from oblivion and presented them to the world with sufficient literary embellishment to make them really attractive reading." The *Preston Herald*, May 9th, 1891, says:—" Mr. W. Pilkington, of this town, has just given to the world his long-promised work on Preston Methodism —its peoples, chapels, and progress—in which he recounts with earnest pen the storms, persecutions, and revivals which the religious denomination of which he is so faithful and ardent an adherent has witnessed. The book is a well-printed demy octavo of nearly 300 pages."

The *Manchester Guardian*, May 12th, 1891, says: —" This book fulfils all that its title promises. It is a plain, full, and very detailed account of the progress of Methodism in Preston from the beginning to the present time. Preston is known to be the Mecca of the teetotal movement, and Mr. Pilkington makes us acquainted with its pioneers. The progress of Methodism in the North of England is illustrated by the diminishing size of the circuits. Among the pioneers of temperance Mr. Pilkington claims the first place for Mr. Henry Anderton, while the palm for strong convincing eloquence is assigned to Mr. James Teare, the first advocate. Those who remember listening to Mr. Teare will agree with all that is here said in his praise. In compiling this volume Mr. Pilkington probably had his Preston neighbours chiefly in view, but it contains some things which will be equally interesting elsewhere."

The *Christian Miscellany*, September, 1891, says:— " We are always glad to see local Methodist histories, for only by their means can we hope to preserve the memory of good and noble men and women whose lives were little known outside their own circle. This volume contains much that is very interesting in regard both to Methodism and Teetotalism in Preston and its neighbourhood. A little compression would have improved the story, but we are pleased to have it as it is."

The *Alliance News*, June 26th, 1891, says:— "This book contains much information about the history of Wesleyan Methodism in North Lancashire, of which many will no doubt be glad to be possessed, It must have required much diligence in its collection. Although 'the Temperance Movement' (by which *we* mean 'the Teetotal Movement') was not welcomed or furthered by some of the leaders of the Connexion in its early days, it received noble help from others, and their fidelity to a good principle and practice has been rewarded by a great growth of true temperance sentiment in the denomination at large. The book contains many portraits of the earlier Methodist preachers, leaders, and others, as well as views of several of their meeting houses."

The *Methodist Temperance Magazine*, August, 1891, says:—" This book is enriched by a preface from the pen of the Rev. Charles Garrett, and is a deeply interesting record of Methodist work in a locality which will always be classic ground for teetotallers. There is much in the book to interest every Methodist and teetotaller."

The *Liverpool Daily Post*, November 25th, 1891, says:—"'The Makers of Preston Methedism,' by W. Pilkington, with a preface by the Rev. Charles Garrett. (Published by the author, 101, Friargate, Preston.) At a meeting of the committee appointed to prepare for celebrating the jubilee of Wesley Chapel, Preston, in November, 1888, Mr. Pilkington was requested to prepare a paper on Preston Methodism from its introduction into the town to the year 1838. The paper he read in connection with the jubilee festivities, and was thereupon desired to bring down the history to the present time, and print it in enlarged form. This he has now done, with the result that he has compiled a most interesting and useful volume, which will be heartily welcome, not only to Methodists in Preston and the neighbourhood, but to all who are attracted by the study of social and religious movements in their earliest developments. Commencing, as a Prestonian was bound to do, with some account of the 'proud town' itself, the author traces the growth of a remarkable religious feeling amongst the untrained and brutal classes of the eighteenth century, from the time of John Wesley's first visit to Preston onward to the establishment of numerous societies and the building of numerous chapels. Needless to say that the opening chapters abound with stories of mob-violence and outrage. It remains eternally true that the people stone the Prophets. In 1784, for instance, a certain Roger Crane, guilty of the heinous crime of being a local preacher, was being dragged along the ground by an infuriated mob who swore they would drown him, and who were setting about their task with as little concern as though it was a mouse they wanted to drown, when he was rescued by a brawny pugilist, who had heard of his charity to the Preston poor. The progress of Methodism is illustrated by capitally executed views of the chapels in the district, and by a number of photographs of its illustrious pioneers. Not the least valuable portion of the work is that which deals with the relation of the early days of the temperance movement to Methodist activity. Without seeking to detract from the honour paid to the famous 'Seven Men of Preston,' renowned in teetotal story, Mr. Pilkington makes good the claim of various Methodist preachers to high rank in the esteem of the Reform party. Abundant statistical information and useful official and historical lists of officers, committees, and the like, complete a handy and readable volume."

WHAT THE MINISTERS SAY.

The Ex-president of the Conference and Chairman of the Liverpool District says :—

"Liverpool, October 20th, 1891.

"Dear Sir,—I have read your handsome volume with great interest. I am especially glad that you have so completely vindicated the temperance movement from being originated by infidels. The book will enrich any library.—I am, yours truly,

"Mr. Pilkington."   "CHARLES GARRETT.

The Rev. Jas. Pratt, superintendent of Lune-street Circuit, Preston, says :—

"3, Jordan-street, Preston,

"26th October, 1891.

"Dear Mr. Pilkington,—In your book entitled 'The Makers of Wesleyan Methodism in Preston' you have brought together a great mass of most interesting and valuable materials. It may be supposed that your history will appeal most strongly to the inhabitants of this district. But there is much in your book of far wider importance —facts which deserve the deep attention of all who care for social progress and national honour. It would be a great advantage to our Church that your book should be generally read and pondered by all our workers throughout our whole Connexion. It is to be feared that many interesting details belonging to the sacrifices and struggles of our noble Methodist fathers and spiritual ancestors are fast passing into oblivion. We cannot afford to lose these stirring records. The public owes a good deal to anyone who sets himself to collect and preserve them. Your work must have been heavy, and can only have been carried through as a labour of love. I trust you will meet with ample success in your publication and sale, and am glad to do what little I can to recommend your book.—I am, yours truly,

"JAMES PRATT."

The Rev. Walter Briscombe, superintendent of Wesley Circuit, Preston, says :—

"1, Peel-terrace, Preston,
"Oct. 23rd, 1891.

"Dear Mr. Pilkington,—Your book gives a most interesting account of the heroic evangelists who founded and built up Preston Methodism, and also relates, in graphic style, the successive developments of its work in the town and neighbourhood. It is pleasantly interspersed with references to characters, customs, and events of general interest which range over the period recorded, and give the book a wider value than its title would indicate. The large section of the book that records the origin of the Temperance Movement, and forcibly sketches the men who organised and pioneered it, should have a special interest for all Temperance Reformers. It is only a just honour to their memories that history should record their noble deeds. It is gratifying to know, on the well-established evidence adduced, that these good men, whose hearts were aglow with zeal to rescue men from the vice of intemperance, had first been penetrated with the influences of the Christian Religion. It is no slight honour to the Methodist Church that so many of her local preachers, and at least one of her Ministers—the Rev. Chas. Radcliffe—rendered such hearty service in the first stages of the movement. It is highly satisfactory to know that the Christian Churches in general have so fully endorsed the enterprise of those who first unofficially pledged to it their Christian support. I wish your book that success which its importance merits, and trust that it may revive and extend that Christian devotion and social benevolence of which it writes such a noble historic chapter.--I am, dear Mr. Pilkington, sincerely yours,

"WALTER BRISCOMBE."

Published by the Author, W. Pilkington, 101, Friar gate, Preston. Price 3s. 6d. ; post free, 3s. 10d.

LIFE SKETCH OF THE REV. WALTER BRIS-
COMBE : By W. Pilkington. With Portrait,
1s. 6d.; being the record of a life distinguished
by a steady devotion to philanthropy and
Christian duty; with the most interesting incidents of his career in eleven circuits.

KEEP STRAIGHT, NELLIE; By W. Pilkington.
Price, 1d.

The *Preston Chronicle* says:—" A practical address,
and shows most vividly the greatness and the grand-
ness of honesty and straightforwardness, illustrating
its meaning by the memorable scaffold saying, 'Keep
Straight, Nellie.'"

TRIED: By W. Pilkington. Price, 1d.

The *Preston Guardian* says:—"An earnest address,
exhorting the boys to practice all those virtues which
make a true and manly life. Illustrated with
capital anecdotes."

The *Preston Herald* says:—"The address teems
with most excellent advice given in a very attractive
and telling form."

HADES, HEAVEN, AND GEHENNA (OR HELL):
By the Rev. Walter Briscombe. With a Controversial Lecture. Price, 2s. 6d.

———

The above works may be had from W. PILKINGTON,
101, Friargate, Preston.